TUNE OF TERROR

TUNE OF TERROR

John St. Robert

Writers Club Press
New York Lincoln Shanghai

Tune of Terror

All Rights Reserved © 2002 by JOHN ST. ROBERT

No part of this book may be reproduced or transmitted in any form or by any means, graphic, electronic, or mechanical, including photocopying, recording, taping, or by any information storage retrieval system, without the written permission of the publisher.

Writers Club Press
an imprint of iUniverse, Inc.

For information address:
iUniverse, Inc.
2021 Pine Lake Road, Suite 100
Lincoln, NE 68512
www.iuniverse.com

ISBN: 0-595-26356-9

Printed in the United States of America

Thanks to my family for their help and to my former associates in the news media who gave me memories to help craft this story.

CHAPTER 1

The honeymoon was over much too soon for Mr. and Mrs. Joseph Kavinsky. Almost immediately upon carrying his blushing bride Sarah over the threshold into their plush wedding suite, the detective noticed a flashing red light. Like an intruder, it interrupted their plans of marital bliss and signaled a message was on the phone next to the beckoning bed awaiting the impatient lovers. Covers were already turned down and mints placed on pillows snuggled up to each other.

The message however left both in virtual shock and disbelief. It was from the port authority of Hamilton, the capital of the island of Bermuda where the newlyweds flew for their honeymoon. The commanding voice delivering the message was from a Bermuda official notifying them of the suicide of Sarah's father, Zack Crimmons. What added to the shock, was that the tragedy happened near the shores of Elbow Beach—the very romantic resort they selected for a wonderful out-of-the way love affair after a gala wedding celebration attended by nearly every cop and reporter in their hometown of St. Paul, Minnesota.

The brief voice-mail left a number to call to receive the sad details. Joe figured the authorities found them by checking over the passport information they gave to Bermuda Customs upon arriving at this British colony. Zack apparently left his name and family information also at Customs when landing there. But little did Sarah know that her father also selected this same small area of the island as a hideaway where he boarded a cruise ship and leaped to his death in the cold North Atlantic.

The last time the couple had any word of Zack was that he was a fugitive fleeing from the Drug Enforcement Agency (DEA). Although he was abusive and very neglectful to his wife and identical twin daughters, Sarah and Susan, Sarah still seemed close to her "daddy." After all, she and her sister were all the relatives left in his family, she reasoned. Her mom, Alice, died a mysterious death that was attributed indirectly to the fact that her husband was connected to a network of drug traffickers around the world and Alice apparently knew too much about this to live. Sarah recalled that her mother's death also was at first ruled a suicide. Alice's body was found slumped in her car one day with the engine running. It appeared she did herself in, until an autopsy revealed a mysterious needle puncture terrorists sometimes used for instant death.

Upon visiting Customs, Joe and Sarah learned more about Zack's fatal plunge and, they were told, the drug-money that went down with him. Feeling guilty not being at home to be with relatives and the few friends paying last respects to Zack, the disappointed couple cut their honeymoon short to return to St. Paul. Moreover, they also had the very unpleasant task of informing Sarah's sister about the grim details.

Her sister was still being held in a police detention center in the Twin Cities awaiting sentencing for allegedly conspiring with a boyfriend, Frank Meyers, a hit man for the drug lords and "Irish Mafia" He was killed while trying to assassinate Joe to find Zack's drug money. Kavinsky became his determined police pursuer, causing Meyers to drown while attempting to escape from Joe on a snowmobile across thin, melting ice on one of the Twin Cities' beautiful, but only partially frozen lakes as winter approached.

The flight back home for the newlyweds was depressing compared to the anticipated glee they experienced enroute to Bermuda. Shortly after landing at the Minneapolis/St. Paul airport, the couple unlocked the door of their new rented home and began unpacking. Sweet memories of the brief honeymoon were still interrupted by somber thoughts of Crimmons jumping off the ship. But Zack, aware that authorities were closing in on him and also despondent and guilty over the treatment he had given to his wife and daughters, apparently decided that drowning was the only way out.

Unfortunately, however, and still unknown by any of Zack's friends or shady associates, much of the money he stole from his drug trafficking went with him to the ocean depths wrapped in heavy bags. Some was earmarked for a few of his fellow mobsters who figured he would share it with them and when he didn't they were enraged. But before he leaped, he wrote checks to his daughters in an attempt to win back their love and forgiveness.

Sarah nor anyone else really knew, nor would they probably ever, that Zack's checks for his daughters never reached their hands. Instead, the checks, scribbled and mailed out just before Zack's plunge, went up in smoke while being delivered in a mail truck that caught fire and nearly burned to the ground a few blocks from where their wedding reception was being held. Postal authorities in St. Paul were still investigating the incident.

Along with still unopened gifts, the unpacking honeymooners had new cards and letters of good wishes to read upon their return home. In addition, there also was a variety of photos to look over, of course, taken by amateur and professional photographers at both the wedding and reception. Like typical lovers, they laughed at times while viewing the silly and romantic photos, some quite candid and, indeed, a few even embarrassing.

But two of the wedding photos especially caught their eyes. These were rather mysterious and came in an envelope with no return address. The envelope was just marked "private" with some shaky scribbling as though written by a very old or handicapped person. Since the anthrax scare, the couple was at first rather hesitant to open the mysterious envelope, especially since it was addressed to a Mr. and Mrs. Joesph Barrott. Surprised, Joe looked twice at the last name and very cautiously opened one end of the envelope. He even shook the envelope to find out if it contained anything like white powder that could indicate anthrax.

Since only a very select few of Joe's closest police associates knew that Barrot was the undercover name Kavinsky used to help capture drug traffickers around the Bahamas recently, he also carefully removed the photos and studied each one closely. There were only three—all, however, somewhat out of focus.

He tried using a magnifying glass to help reveal the sender's name without success, but could only detect some tiny scribbling on a corner in back of each picture—including one showing him slipping the wedding ring on Sarah's finger.

After much squinting and determination, Kavinsky finally pieced together some words on back of the photos. One read: *"taken with Barrot's camera at Bimini security station."* On the second, showing Sarah's sister escorted by a marshal at the wedding prior to her being arraigned as an accomplice in drug trafficking, was scrawled *"good riddance".* The third, showing Joe and Sarah being toasted at the reception, was the most interesting however. It read in big black letters: **"Will be getting in touch with you soon…with your camera."**

"Hey, honey, guess what? We might be getting our old camera back—you know, the one inscribed with a heart that I gave you?—it hasn't been stolen after all." Scratching his head, he wondered out loud, "But who the hell took these pictures? The drug smugglers ran off with this camera in the Bahamas."

"Are you sure they were taken by our camera?" asked Sarah snuggling up to her tanned, muscular husband. "We certainly didn't invite anyone from the Bahamas." She fondly remembered, though, that Joe gave her the camera as a birthday present and then borrowed it for some photos he needed to take when he was in pursuit of the smugglers.

"Yeah—this is really strange. I recall exactly when those two tough security guys at the airport check-in counter took it from me."

Scratching his head again, he added: "They were part of the Beck gang checking out recruits. But how did they get to our wedding—and pass airport security—and why would they bother to send me these pictures?"

"Do you suppose you should notify your pals at the Drug Enforcement Agency?" asked Sarah, especially nervous since the 9/11 terrorist tragedy.

"Wouldn't hurt—maybe Terry Johnson could give me an idea on how to handle this." It seemed like only a few weeks ago that Joe and Terry, a member of the DEA, had successfully escaped the elusive drug lord Robert Beck from his hidden headquarters in Bimini, where much of Beck's illegal drugs were being flown to the U.S. heartland as well as to many other parts of the world.

"After all, I did agree to be one of their undercover guys," noted Joe.

He also recalled consenting to assist the DEA while returning home in one of their planes after helping to catch some of the narcotic smugglers as they attempted to make a drug run to the Twin Cities.

He also knew he had to be especially discreet about this and almost swore Sarah to secrecy since he also was still a detective for the St. Paul police department. But he now had two "bosses" to report to—one, the new police chief, Fred Hermes, who replaced the former chief Neil Cermak, after Cermak was accused of conspiring with drug traffickers but escaped arrest. The other was Terry Johnson—who the DEA chose as their special agent to help protect the U.S. from drugs coming in from offshore islands, including the Bahamas as well as from many other international bases.

While Sarah busied herself with carefully putting away wedding memorabilia, Joe looked up Terry's phone number in his little note book that went everywhere the detective went. The number was unlisted, however, and couldn't be traced. But Joe had received it personally from Johnson, who trusted him like a brother. He realized Joe would probably even swallow information he received from the DEA rather than pass it on to anyone not on their recommended list.

Like most phone calls to federal law enforcement organizations, the caller is first identified via special caller-ID, enabling the person receiving the call to check the source before acknowledging it. Joe knew Terry well enough, however, to be confident his voice would be recognized and that his call would immediately be taken seriously, even though the name on the phone monitor came up "*JOKE*". Both kidded about this since it was short for Joe Kavinsky. Adding to the credibility of the call, of course, would be the DEA reference number Joe was given by Terry. His ID was simply "*TJ*" when responding to Joe's calling him on their security call phones.

This special code system also let Joe know that Johnson would call him Back ASAP—that is, if Johnson was by the phone, which was rather unlikely since Terry could already be on the other side of the globe catching bad guys. Despite all this, Joe calmly dialed his covert friend with hopes of hearing from him sooner than later.

Believing it would be later—much later—Joe went back to helping Sarah find room for their wedding gifts. But no sooner had he put the phone down than it began ringing, almost startling Joe and his bride. Sure enough, the caller-ID came up with the letters"*TJ*".

"Joe old boy, wassup?" asked Johnson in his cool way.

Kavinsky began by telling him about the strange note and photos he received, apparently from someone who was involved in stealing his camera while he was being frisked by a Beck security guard. The same guy must have been taking photos at his wedding, Joe concluded.

Much to Joe's amazement he heard Terry casually reply, "Oh sure, I know that dude—he's one of ours."

"What do you mean, one of ours?" asked the surprised Kavinsky. The guy with the mustache at the check-in counter—remember?

"Sort of, but everything seemed rather panicky for me at the time."

"Yeah—and rightly so. But if it wasn't for him that gun you were hiding from security would have ended up in your butt instead of your shoe."

"How did you know I had it in my shoe? No one looked in them."

"That's cause my guy let you get through—he kept an eye on you letting us know the moment you arrived and where you'd be staying. At the Pilot Knob wasn't it?" Surprised at such recall, Joe asked, "who is he, and what's his name?. I thought those guys were just a bunch of Beck hooligans."

"For the sake of our security and his protection, let's just say he's 'My Guy'. If you see him, call him that. We don't want to blow his cover."

"And you should very definitely see My Guy...He's very important to us Joe. I can't go into details, but he may be leading us to get the big guy—if you get what I mean—and also maybe catch some Al-Qaida terrorists along the way."

After telling Kavinsky he would fill him in more when they get together, Terry suggested that they meet for lunch in a spot where they could mostly be unnoticed. Kavinsky chuckled over this since he and his uncle Al, the local police reporter, always seemed to be the last to be noticed at Maxi's near the newspaper office, especially when the fashion models would strut their stuff at lunch as Joe and Al talked police-reporter matters. Some, however, winked at the handsome young detective while strolling by.

"Good, why not Maxi's at noon tomorrow?" suggested Joe.

"Sounds okay, I understand they have some good entertainment, too," Terry responded, letting Joe know he's been there before looking at the ladies.

"You ole dawg," laughed Joe, heckling Terry, knowing his interest in the feminine sex.

"No—but you may be...let's say you may even be our hound dog," Terry said seriously.

CHAPTER 2

Although Kavinsky spoke softly, Sarah overheard some of the phone conversation between Joe and Terry, especially about Maxi's and the models.

"You and those peep show luncheons. I thought you and your uncle had enough of those for awhile," she said teasingly—like a jealous bride.

"I have to keep my eyes open, honey," explained Joe. "It's getting kinda spooky out there. That camera thing seems real weird. I'll know more when meeting Johnson again, and what I may be doing for him. He called me his hound dog—but I have a feeling I'll be more like his blood hound."

Although still slightly fatigued from arranging furniture and finding room for all the "loot" from their wedding, Joe was up early the next morning to get his mind somewhat organized to talk with his snoop friend Johnson.

But he first had to report in at the local police precinct and review some reports left while he was gone for his honeymoon. The new chief still wanted him to check out reports of embezzlement on the north end, much like Cermak had him do.

Since Maxi's was right around that area, it was rather convenient for Kavinsky to stop off there, although he knew it was designed mostly for young dudes looking for some possible easy pickups.

However, Joe ignored much of this since he realized he was now a respectable married man and only there looking for his friend Johnson. And he also realized that in Terry's type of work he could have many disguises.

Fortunately, Terry had already grabbed a table on the sidelines amid all the swarming flirtatious bodies, and was easy to spot as Joe looked about.

He was rather surprised that Johnson had no beard, sunglasses or any other additions that might change his appearance. After all, in this place a few pierced body parts, on the tongue, nose, navel or elsewhere would be most appropriate.

Terry was sitting with someone else, though, who fit in better with more of this swinging crowd. He had a curvy mustache, a dangling pony tail and big forced smile.

"Hey Joe, I'd like you to meet My Guy," said Johnson pointing to the large black dude seated next to him.

"We've already met mon," said the mustached one rising to shake hands with Joe.

"I understand we have—in the Bahamas wasn't it?"

"I thought you'd like your camera back Joe Barrott—or should I say Kavinsky?" chuckled My Guy.

"Where's your pal that frisked me down to my socks?" asked Joe neglecting to smile back.

"Ah, but not to your shoes mon where you had your gun," reminded My Guy, with an even wider grin. Without further adieu, My Guy returned Joe his old beloved camera as Terry's expression also changed from frowning to smiling.

"Sit down Joe, Terry commanded. "My Guy is definitely off his turf but if anyone caught him with us it may too bad for all of us." He quipped," I left my mask at home…most of those here, however, seem to be looking for skirts."

"Most, yeah," Joe half-heartedly agreed while peering around the lounge area. Terry continued, "here's the scoop, as your reporter uncle would say, we need you to cooperate with My Guy. He knows about every move Beck takes—here, in the Bahamas and even where lots of drugs are grown in Colombia and the Mideast.

As you know, the FBI, CIA, HOME SECURITY as well as DEA, have all been trying to catch up with Beck. He's a kingpin and as slippery as an eel. I also know there are very few around here as familiar as you are with his Bahama base of operations. Hell, you saw him almost face-to-face and I recall nearly bumped into him."

"And so?...," Joe shrugged urging Johnson on as to how he fits in to all this.

"So, we're laying a trap for Beck. The word from My Guy here is that he's coming to the Midwest,—our town—the Twin Cities, believe it or not. Just think, this S.O.B. has been giving us the slip for years. He's as notorious as Osama bin Laden and al Qaida. But we actually think we can get him this time Joe—with your help."

With that, Joe quickly put up his hand to halt the conversation.

"For God's sake Terry—I just got married and still have duties to perform for my new police chief."

"We know that. But we figure if all goes well we should have Beck very soon. We already know his trip plans. My Guy also knows Beck like the back of his hands. He's been a security guard for him for years—he's very good at that as you know. We can give you all the support you want.

"And don't worry about the chief, DEA has already been in touch with him and he's agreeable to letting you loose on this—without any loss of salary or seniority," Johnson added with a wry grin.

"And how about my wife—did you already get an okay from her?" asked Joe sarcastically "Don't tell her—no one else should know. It'll work out, trust us.

"From what I hear you've always been very good at charming the ladies. We pay very well you know. She can shop and buy lots of things," Terry added with a chuckle.

"You do, huh?" responded Joe. "How do I know this is going to be quick, and how risky is it?"

"If everything goes right, it may be quicker than we think. Hell Joe we have that drug lord almost pinned down now. Once you see our plan, you'll know how to help bring him in. Why he's coming here or how, we're not sure yet, but we do know he's coming for no damn good. God, Joe, this guy is Mr. Evil himself.

"We picked you since you're not officially labeled with any federal authorities. You told me in the Bahamas that you even saw the colors of his eyes and studied his mannerisms but that he never spotted you. My Guy will always stay in the background. Beck still trusts him—meaning he'll be able to continue giving you some great inside information. But if they catch on, they'll do their utmost to get in your way."

Assuring Johnson that he'd seriously think about it, Kavinsky returned to his new love nest. While trying to catch up on some of the many newspapers piled up while he was out of the country, he couldn't help but read about all the drug smuggling and terrorism going on in the U.S. and abroad. The slogan: "Drug Money Supports Terror" and 9/11 memories seen so often on TV, also helped him decide to go along with the DEA to help stop this from spreading further—especially in Joe's home state already hit hard with drugs.

Informing Johnson of his decision by way of the DEA's super phone security system, Joe was reminded by Terry once more of not telling anyone about this undercover work—called *BAR* for "Beat Addict Runners". In fact, he warned Joe again not to discuss it, even with his fellow cops, except for the new chief who was informed of it. He said some of Beck's cell mates may already know of Joe's whereabouts and do anything to keep him from spoiling plans to get their leader back into this country.

Realizing that keeping anything secret from Sarah was nearly impossible, considering their lovey-dovey relationship, Kavinsky purposely kept busy like a good husband should helping with home improvements, including painting walls and trimming the hedge, knowing in only a few more days he would be busy with BAR.

To take a break from this housework, Sarah suggested they go to what is considered the nation's largest indoor shopping center, the megamall, in suburban Minneapolis. Joe agreed rather begrudgingly to tag along. Ever since the World Trade Center tragedy, all of its entrances were barricaded by huge concrete containers to discourage possible terrorists from ramming the great merchandise mecca with explosives. Moreover, police were now even bicycling outside the place to help spot suspicious characters while police dogs sniffed around, with many of them inside to also protect against suicide bombers.

Like most visitors to this gigantic mall, Sarah and Joe also took in some of its many special entertainment activities, including super thrill rides, and even visited Camp Goofy. Joe brought his camera, but only to get it fixed. It didn't work since getting it back from My Guy. He could hardly walk after experiencing a ride that was mostly upside down while twirling near the rafters of the multi-story retail complex.

CHAPTER 3

It was almost by luck that Kavinsky and Sarah were able to find a nearby coffee shop for a latte to get more relaxed, and to figure out directions to where the hell they should be off to next.

But, guided by her feminine shopping instincts, Sarah in no way wanted to dawdle long at the coffee counter, and urged her anti-shopping husband to continue making the retail rounds of the huge mall.

In addition to the swarm of fellow shoppers they encountered they also had to dodge around many serious walkers getting in their daily exercise. You could easily spot them, wearing their white shoes and moving their arms up and down in rhythm with each brisk step. Many were "ma-and-pa" types walking as fast as they can, ignoring the window displays. Although Joe saw some of the old guys sneaking peeks at the near naked mannequins boldly displayed in the windows of Victoria's Secret.

It was while weaving in and out of this heavy traffic, trying not to spill their coffee, that they almost bumped into a group of mall visitors looking for someone to take a picture of them in front of one of the unique shops on the third floor.

Considering that many come to this mall from far-off places of the world, Joe wasn't too surprised when one of the group, a young woman, who you could tell was beautiful even though her face was partially hidden by a Mideast face scarf, approached him. She asked if he would be kind enough to take a photo of them in front of a rather strange restaurant with a stuffed gorilla at the entranceway.

Kavinsky figured they asked him since he also looked like a tourist, still wearing his straw hat from the Bahamas. They had some sort of foreign insta-matic camera, resembling a Polaroid. He received it from the very friendly, courteous, and half-masked young lady who apparently was the group's spokesperson,

This group was a real mix, thought Joe. Both big and small, white and black. Most of the women had nearly all or most of their faces covered and many of the guys wore beards dating back to Bible days. They all smiled for the camera, however, as Joe stepped back near a railing looking down on the immense mall interior to get everyone in the picture. Luckily, he wasn't using his large camera since he'd probably fall over the railing trying to focus it. Sarah finished her latte and, since she had so many shopping bags, the group leader offered to hold Joe's coffee cup while he shot the photo.

After several photos were taken, Joe handed the camera back to the scarfed lady. He noted she had a robe slit on the side revealing sexy legs and that she passed his cup to a man behind her. After thanking Joe and returning his coffee the weird group proceeded on, marveling at more unusual eye-catching shops along the way.

"I'm sorry I didn't get a look at those photos. Those Polaroids can really come up with some quick prints. But that gal apparently was in a rush," shrugged Joe. Sarah kidded him about his attention over such a "pretty little thing," as they inspected a pedometer on her belt showing the number of steps needed for her daily workout. While gazing at this on the next level, they suddenly met the group again.

In somewhat broken English, the Muslim lady humbly excused herself for asking Joe to take another picture. She explained that those he took earlier didn't turn out for some reason, and would he "please, please" retake them.

"We'll hold your coffee for you again," she offered with a somewhat flirting smile. In fact, Joe thought she may have even winked at him.

"Sure, I'll take it right away," he said to get them on their way.

She asked smilingly, "How do you like your coffee? I understand they make it very good here" He replied, "Fine, I guess…haven't had much of it yet though," indicating he was being interrupted too often. "You may want a taste." He then noticed that she passed the cup once more to someone to hold in the background.

In fact, after they left and he got his coffee back, Joe figured he didn't even have a swig of it before meeting up with that group. But it felt cold by now and uninteresting, so he and Sarah looked for a container to toss it into. He kept holding it, however, until leaving. Noticing one of the big cement containers directly next to the front door with some flowers peeping out, he tossed the rest of his coffee into it. About a second later he almost reached for his gun as Sarah began screaming.

"Oh, my God Joe," gasped Sarah so loudly and with so much fright that Joe nearly stumbled. "Look what you've done to those beautiful flowers…you killed them." Startled, Kavinsky stood with his mouth open feeling guilty and stunned as he watched the flowers wither away, almost pleading for help.

CHAPTER 4

"What the hell was in that stuff anyway?" asked Kavinsky as he looked at the dead flowers, which a few moments ago were attracting passersby with their very vibrant colors that helped disguise the huge containers serving as barricades in front of the mall. "It sure was more than a skim latte."

"It must be highly toxic. It's a miracle you didn't drink it."

"I didn't want any after getting it back from that strange bunch."

"Do you think they put something in it?"

"Could be—I'm going back to see them," declared Joe.

"No Joe, don't", pleaded Sarah. "What if they did have something to do with it…they would probably try to harm you."

"Naw—I still carry a gun, remember. I'll only be gone a short time.

You go home. I'll notify you on my cell phone."

"But the coffee's gone, it's already absorbed into the dirt. How can you prove anything?" Sarah wondered.

"I still have my cup…our investigators might be able to get some evidence from it—fingerprints, who knows what those clever guys of ours can find. After all, the head gal or her buddies may have sampled it…there's still some residue at the bottom of the cup."

With that, Joe sped off—past the big container barricades, through the shoe department overloaded with sales racks, and even ran up the escalators, skipping every other step, as he rushed to the mall's top floor almost to the tune of the piano music being played on the first floor for shopper entertainment.

He knew exactly where he was standing with the camera, but when he got there the "groupies" were nowhere in sight. He then rushed back to the down-escalator to get to the second floor where the first picture was taken. It was when he was running alongside the railing in hot pursuit that he nearly got bumped off. He didn't see the person he collided with while trying to dodge between all the shoppers, but he was so close to hitting the railing and falling that for a second or so he was sure he was going to hit the hard marble floor below and crack like an egg. He could have sworn that the guy who bumped him resembled someone in that group he photographed. But, of course, those guys had the pictures—so there was no proof of anything. Besides, Joe thought, his imagination may be running wild recalling his warnings from Johnson.

All the young detective knew for certain was that he still grasped the coffee cup and could bring it to the crime lab as fast as he could get there.

"What the hell do you think was in this stuff? "asked Joe when talking to George Reed, head of the forensic lab. "It killed those plants outside the mall instantly. You could almost hear them yell with pain."

"Dunno yet, Joe, but we'll find out. All I can say is you're damn lucky you didn't down any of it. If so, you'd better get a stomach x-ray soon."

CHAPTER 5

Joe did get his stomach checked just in case, but no trace of poison could be found—meaning the poison was put in the cup after he tasted it. "Is there any way you can trace this down?" Kavinsky asked. "My fingerprints are probably all over the cup since I did sip the coffee a little before taking a picture of that group.

They would have also left some prints. One of them was even tasting the coffee."

"Don't know for sure, Joe. But even if we can't, there's a good possibility that there may be a trace of saliva left."

"Meaning what?" questioned Kavinsky. "Meaning even though there's no blood, we can do some DNA work on this. DNA has improved a lot these days.

We can separate your and prints from the other person's. In fact, this would be even better than prints. At least we have a good chance to track down the matching DNA saliva sample," noted the forensic expert.

"While you're doing that, I have a call to make," said Joe, as he dashed off to find a private place to use his cell phone.

Dialing his pal Johnson's DEA code number, Kavinsky received a quick call back. As expected, Terry just responded: "TJ speaking."

"TJ. Just what the hell is going on? I almost swallowed some poison at the mall this morning with my coffee. And it wasn't from the coffee maker. I'm pretty sure it was from a Mideast gang who may be connected to the Beck operation. I think they put something in it."

"Wait Joe, why the hell were you with this gang?" interrupted a slightly confused Terry.

"They wanted a photo taken and I seemed to be the only guy around to take it. They let me use their camera."

"And you in turn let them hold your coffee cup?" quizzed Terry as though knowing what's coming next.

"Exactly. And on my way out of the mall with the cup I tossed some of the ingredients in the plants—almost ruining the barricaded entranceway."

"Wow, you sure lead a charmed life," summed up Johnson.

"It's nothing to kid about, Terry. My question is: is it possible that those photo hogs wanted to kill me because of my connection with your hunt for Beck?"

"Good question Joe. Wish I had a good answer."

He added, "We'd better discuss this privately—just you and me. But this time not in that mob scene at that noisy restaurant you selected."

"How about Toby's, a little secluded place near the campus. I guarantee there's no models hanging out there. Hell, for all I've noticed, it's mostly homely coeds." Even Joe was surprised he was treating this matter so flippantly.

"As long as no-one can spot us together Joe. This has become very serious. I had no idea anyone suspected you were with us."

"If it's a campus crowd I don't see any harm in that. Maybe we can put on our very best 'Goldy Gopher' T-shirts and they'll think we belong to the U of M," quipped Johnson, who like Joe was an ex jock at the university.

"Or reverse our baseball caps like the kids do." Joe chuckled. "But please keep your guy—or whatever you call him—the hell out of this. My gut tells me he doesn't belong."

"You're wrong, Joe. He's one of us. He has a long record of faithful and heroic service and has been sticking his neck out for us as an undercover agent many times."

"Then how do you account for this incident?—both my bride and I could have been killed by that poison coffee. I can't help but tie it in with my role in trying to catch Beck. It's just too much of a coincidence."

"I believe you're right about that. But someone other than My Guy got the word out. Who it is, I don't know at this point. It could be that someone saw us talking at that restaurant of yours—remember the models? Or, it might even be someone in our own organizations, one of your cops or my drug enforcers."

"Hopefully the crime lab will put something together—the DNA may get some connection. It's sure hard to believe the little gal that approached me to take the picture had anything to do with it," Joe shrugged.

"She was just a front," Joe. "At this time I'd say they're trying to scare you off. They're paving the way for the coming of their drug lord and making damn sure that nothing—or anyone—interferes."

"What do we do now?" asked Kavinsky, lighting a cigarette and staring at Johnson.

"Just sit tight and wait for the lab to give you a report. In the meantime, stay away from those latte coffees," Terry said jokingly.

But it seemed like days before the crime lab got back to Joe. Reed had very little to report on his DNA investigation so far when Joe called him.

"We did get some traces of saliva and prints Joe but it's awfully tough to prove anything without a sample to match," he said.

"Yeah, that figures," agreed Joe. "Did you search all your known drug and terrorist files? You know the saying, "drug money and terrorism go together."

"There's just so much to try to match, Joe. And we have so many other cases to investigate. I guess we're going to have to call it off for the time being."

"But George, I'm anxious to know the results. Also if I get any leads I'll be sure to pass them on to you," said the somewhat disappointed detective to the forensic expert.

CHAPTER 6

After Joe hung up, he looked at the calendar above his computer and suddenly realized he was to resume his job with his local police precinct on the 9:30 a.m. to 6.30 p.m.shift. Although he had that date circled in big red ink, he was so busy snooping for the DEA that he almost forgot this commitment with the St. Paul cops.

Joe fit into his old work routine smoothly, with several projects marked on his assignment sheet by his reliable secretary Liz. But before he could start anything he was buzzed by chief Hermes. Joe noticed the chief was very careful to close his door when Joe entered as if to make sure no one heard what would be said.

Hermes, who Joe considered a good cop well-deserving of promotion upon the mysterious departure of chief Cermak, stood up from his desk and shook Kavinsky's hand vigorously. Joe was relieved since he wasn't sure how all his running around in the Bahamas to catch drug thieves went over with his hometown colleagues.

After further reassuring Joe of his support with a big smile, the new chief congratulated Kavinsky and informed him that a large pay raise was forthcoming for his keen detective work. Joe's response was "Great! wait 'til Sarah hears about this. She'll sure be on a shopping spree."

"You've done a fine job, Joe. You've always been a dedicated cop and determined pursuer. I'm also happy to hear that you've accepted a temporary undercover job for the DEA. We're always proud that one of our own can help the feds when possible. I recommended you highly."

He added, "By the way how's it going with your DEA program? No one else around here knows about this, of course."

"It's going fine, chief. But just recently it seems some spy work may be going on by a person or persons within the DEA or even our own police department."

"You mean a mole?" asked the surprised chief, sitting down.and beginning to frown.

"Could be. But we're not sure. As you know Cermak escaped arrest and no one really knows where he is. It may be that one of his old buddies on the force does. Perhaps even someone who wouldn't hesitate to do away with anyone who wants to catch Cermak."

"Any suspects yet?" asked Hermes lighting a cigar and reclining back in his captain's chair indicating he wanted more information.

"I'm hoping maybe you can help me find one or two chief."

"You playing some hunches Joe?"

"Could be—maybe around our precinct."

"This place isn't bugged Joe. Tell me if there's any monkey business going on here…give it to me straight."

Joe got up from his chair and lit another cigarette. With a frown, he told Hermes about the near-death incident with his coffee cup at the mall, and the attempt by the lab to help identify the culprit by matching DNA samples.

"So how do I relate to any of this Joe?"

"Let's face it chief, as long as Cermak is still alive he could be among us in disguise or even have one of his many pals around our precinct to do a hit.

"The only pals he may have had are Dave Paulson and maybe one or two others. And they seem clean. I know we'd spot a suspect if he, or she, was close."

"For that matter, it may be someone in the Bahamas with Beck. But I won't bore you further chief. I'll also keep my eyes and ears open."

Upon departing the chief's office, Kavinsky walked down the stairs to the precinct's restaurant for a snack. He was surprised to bump into his old nemesis Paulson enjoying some java and a bun at one of the restaurant tables while talking with Jeff, the crime sketch artist.

"Well, ain't this a coincidence," remarked Paulson for openers on seeing Joe.

"Too much so," responded Kavinsky. "Haven't seen Jeff since he drew a sketch for me of Sloan the druggie," referring to Zack's late conspirator in drug smuggling who was identified by one of Jeff's sketches.

Pouring some coffee from Dave's jug into an empty cup on the table, Joe asked Paulson how thing's were going, and if anyone figured out where the hell the ex police chief was hiding out these days.

"Very funny...you know as much or more about that than I do," shrugged Paulson. "Maybe Jeff here can draw a picture of him from memory and spin a bottle as to where he might be."

Joe didn't laugh back. Paulson got him thinking that perhaps the artist indeed could sketch what Joe could recall about the woman who asked him to take that group picture in the megamall. After all, he remembered she was the cutest of the bunch.

His thoughts were interrupted, however, when one of the rookie cops sat down and also helped himself to Paulson's coffee pot. He had just been assigned to work with Dave. Before Paulson could say "Do you mind?" the newcomer took a couple of drinks, asked "what's up" and started to join in on their conversation.

Getting cold stares from both Paulson and Kavinsky let the rookie—who Dave introduced as Amad—clearly know that he wasn't wanted. He quickly took one more swig of coffee, left his cup on the table, and took off.

Taking a look at his watch, Joe also thought it time to leave. He offered to take the empty coffee cups to the conveyor for cleaning along with the dirty snack dishes on his way out. But just before placing them on the conveyor the thought came to him to send them onto the lab for saliva testing. He shrugged and mumbled to himself "why not?"

Later in the day Joe also began working with the artist. But sketching the girl who asked him to take those photos took longer than expected. It was difficult for Kavinsky to describe her vividly enough since her face was partially covered by a scarf. He tried to recall her main features as the artist began doodling each time Joe came up with an extra detail.

After about a dozen attempts, one of the sketches seemed to be the best. Joe asked for several copies and advised the artist to file the others carefully. He then went home and had Sarah confirm that this indeed was very close to what the group leader looked like. "All I can remember was she was very cute," Joe kidded.

The next day Kavinsky was in his squad car and found himself once more only a few miles from the super mall. He couldn't help but wonder if that gang of photo hounds was there again, and perhaps with any luck he could find them.

Knowing there was a good chance he could search around the mall without disturbing his new chief, he once again went through the main entrance—noticing that the dead flowers had been removed from the container he tossed his coffee into. All that remained was a tiny plant vainly trying to emerge from the disturbed dirt where beauty once bloomed.

CHAPTER 7

Everything seemed the same, as he walked through the main entrance and quickly encountered racks of new shoes on display. Even the same piano player was playing the same song. In fact, as Joe looked at the pianist he was pleasantly surprised to see that it was his old classmate Pete—Pete Paskelli who was always great on the keys.

"Pete—for Pete's sake," said Joe grinning. I always wondered where you ended up. I figured you were playing in Carnegie Hall by now." He used to be known as Piano Pete because of his great musical skills.

"Joe—Joe Kavinsky. The dude who had all the girls buzzing around him. I'm doing this part-time while getting a Phd. from the U here," said the surprised young man behind the baby grand. "What's up with you?"

"I'm now a cop. And to think our grade school teachers said we wouldn't amount to anything," he kidded.

"What are you snooping for around here?" inquired Pete.

"Can't say, my friend. But I sure like that melody you're playing. I met my wife while dancing to that."

"It's amazing how so many passersby ask me to play something that they remember from their romantic days," said the pianist. "Both young and old."

The young part caught Joe's attention. He immediately wondered if Pete might be able to help him catch the young lady who asked him to shoot that picture.

The only thing he had to go by was that sketch from the police artist. He took it from his pocket and showed it to Pete without disclosing why he wanted him to be on the lookout for her.

"How would I know how to contact you if I did see someone like this?" asked Pete with a frown. "Besides I have to be almost constantly playing this piano for my ten-bucks-an-hour."

Joe pondered this for a few moments. The thought struck him, however, after listening to his friend playing so many familiar tunes, that maybe he could come up with an altogether different type melody which would signal when, and if, he spotted someone resembling the sketch, either coming or going.

"Well, if you really, really want to be different I can play 'Santa Claus is Coming to Town'. In mid summer this should get some attention," said Pete jokingly.

"Yeah—I used to hum it a lot as a kid," recalled Joe with a smile, realizing this would be quite appropriate considering 'Beck the Bad' is also coming. Worst yet, he could even be strolling around town already, loading a bag full of drugs.

"Good Joe—you'll be able to hear my piano piped around every level of the main anchor store where I'm playing. If I suddenly start playing 'he's coming to town' you'll know I've spotted your man…oops girl."

With that in mind, Kavinsky showed his piano-playing pal the sketch of the suspect and told him to keep it close to the keys. If he saw anyone like this to immediately go into his wild version of old Santy and his reindeers, even though everyone around the mall may think he's nuts.

"But right now I'm going to continue strolling around like a shopper in case I might bump into that thirsty group again," said Joe.

With that, Kavinsky took off, keeping his eyes and ears wide open for anyone looking like they might belong to that odd bunch. He knew it was a long shot, but who knows how much odd planning goes into protecting a shady ass like Beck. For that matter, the tall thin shopper approaching him could even be bin Laden without a beard. But he was just another sightseer.

For some reason, Joe felt comfortable walking fast even with his gun and cell phone bouncing under his jacket. And although he was nearing the top floor he could still hear Pete pounding the keys. He was playing a cool tune from Brittany as many of the young girls going by in hip-huggers began wiggling to the tune and giggling.

Despite the loud hip-swinging music, however, Kavinsky was still able to clearly hear his cell phone ring. It was George from the crime lab.

"Joe, what do you know. We did find some matching saliva on those couple of coffee cups you gave us."

"It was just a wild guess," explained a surprised Kavinsky. "I really didn't think my side-kick would be involved."

"Maybe he isn't," the lab tech cautioned. "It might be the other person with him. But the only way we can find out for sure is for you to get another culture on one of them."

Joe stood at the top of the escalator as though wondering what to do next. "I'll find a discreet way to do that…and appreciate your keeping very silent about all this."

With George's promise for secrecy, the cop proceeded through the mall. He got only a few yards however when his thoughts of finding a way to get a DNA sample were interrupted by very loud piano music that caused passersby to snicker.

"Damn, there it is…Pete's Santa is coming to town," muttered Joe so loud that some shoppers made it a point to keep their distance from him.

CHAPTER 8

❦

While all this was going on, Al Benjamin, Joe's snoopy reporter uncle was sticking his nose into police matters again. His nephew was sure Al knew nothing about the coming of Beck nor any of the activities going on to catch him. In fact, Kavinsky went out of his way to distract Al by talking about his favorite subjects, hunting and fishing, every time they got together.

It was simply an accident, in more ways than one, that nephew and uncle ran into one another in Joe's mad chase down the escalator to Pete's piano. They collided on the second level just after Kavinsky jumped off the bottom escalator step.

"Uncle Al what the hell you doing here?" was all Joe could utter almost out-of-breath.

"I have to pay one of my wife's bills at the cashier's up here," replied Al wondering what Joe's great rush was all about.

"I can't talk right now unc. I'm after a bad woman."

"But Joe, you're married now. What the hell, get control of yourself man," Al admonished.

"No, I don't mean like that unc. She's tied in with drugs. I gotta catch her, maybe arrest her."

Right then, Joe paused in his chase, realizing that he just tipped off one of the most aggressive reporters in the world a little to what was supposed to be very hushed-up from the press.

"Forget I said that unc. Just let me finish my chase."

"You gotta tell me about it, Joey. You just blew it. I'll step aside but let's talk."

"Okay, okay anything you want. Just get out of my way now unc. She's probably already out the door."

"When can we get together on this?" Al asked not wanting a chance for a scoop to escape."

"In a couple of days—at noon—at Maxi's." Joe responded almost pushing Al aside.

"I'll be there. Good luck in catching whoever it is you're after."

"Thanks, but I think I'm already too late."

He was right. By the time Kavinsky reached the piano area the pianist was pointing to the door nearby indicating that the suspect just got away.

"Joe, I'm sure she was the one. Her face looked almost exactly as your artist drew it," Pete almost yelled. "You're right, she's a real looker with a shape that can't be hidden, even better than Brittany's." Kavinsky wasn't about to discuss it as he quickly dashed to the door, past the big barricades and onto the street. He spent some time looking up and down on both sides of the street and even up on the second-level skywalk again. But alas—his suspect had vanished, perhaps driving the convertible that almost ran him over while screeching its wheels and racing to the freeway. He had to jump to the sidewalk but wasn't able to see the license plate.

Returning home disappointed, Joe told Sarah about running into his uncle and blabbing to him. He was careful not to go into details about his involvement. He merely informed her that he planned to meet Al at lunch soon and talk police matters. She asked if anyone else was joining them. This gave the cop the idea to also invite Paulson in hope of obtaining another saliva sample off whatever cup or glass he might be using.

His thoughts quickly resisted doing this, however, recalling Johnson's warning about keeping this operation super secret. He felt safe, however, in getting together with his trustworthy uncle in a coupe of days.

Joe did make it a point, though, to sit down with Paulson the next day when he broke for lunch in the precinct lounge. The timing couldn't be better.

There was even an empty seat next to his partner. They shot the breeze, mostly about the ex-chief and how he got away from being caught when the feds were hot on his trail.

Neither could figure out how Cermak got the word so fast that allowed him to run and hide. As chummy as this was, Joe wasn't sure even now if Paulson was leveling with him.

Time went fast when talking about that slippery s.o.b. Cermak, both agreed. Despite the hurried lunch, Joe was able to refill Paulson's cup of coffee. As soon as that was downed, Paulson checked his watch and announced he had to rush off. He seemed glad to hear Kavinsky's offer to bring his empty lunch tray and coffee cup to the dirty-dish conveyor so he could be on time for his next assignment.

When Paulson was out-of-sight, however, Joe put the tray on the restaurant conveyor belt, but very carefully grasped the small cup with a towel and put it inside his pocket. He then headed for George in the crime lab with what might help lead to the whereabouts of Beck, although hoping that Dave was clean in all this.

While waiting for George's report, Kavinsky began looking into the background of that rookie who barged into the conversation Joe was having with Paulson the other day at lunch. He wasn't discounting the many clever approaches Beck might be using to assure there would be no obstacles in carrying out his U.S. mission.

"Why the hell does Beck want to come here anyway, Terry?" asked Kavinsky when he got together with him again, this time at a hideaway recommended by Johnson.

"This is what we're asking, too, Joe—at the DEA. Keep in mind that as far as we know, this guy's never had the guts to set his feet back on U.S. turf for fear of immediate imprisonment, or worse, since becoming involved in all this drug trafficking and murder. All I can say is, his visit must be extremely important to him."

"But doesn't he have a wife and family here?"

"They're under our protective custody, Joe. And that's all I can say about that," said Terry, snuffing out his cigarette.

But he added, looking sternly at Joe, "the person we're mostly concerned about right now is you."

"Despite your phony name of Barrott used in the Bahamas, the bad guys know you were the one that spoiled their drug smuggling over here...and that you actually saw Beck. They certainly don't want you to ruin their plans. They're trying to get to you in a very sneaky way—rather than blow you off and create more suspicion.

"My Guy reports that they want a perfect stage for Beck's coming with no interference from anyone. How he comes, or under what name or appearance, is anyone's guess at this point."

Joe interrupted, "But what about My Guy?—isn't he in very big danger?"

"Yeah, and he's over there again in Bimini in the Bahamas—that's why it's so important that neither you nor me, or any others, say or do anything that will jeopardize his situation."

Their conversation was cut short by the jingling of Joe's cell phone.

"And get rid of that damn thing," said Johnson frowning at the phone, "anything that will draw attention to us at our meetings is bad news."

The voice on the other end was George's. It said simply:

"Joe—there's no match."

Terry noticed Kavinsky wiping his brow and waited for Joe to complete the call before saying: "It wasn't Paulson, was it."

"Terry how the hell did you know about this?"

"I keep telling you we've got lots of eyes on you—just in case you need support."

"Do you know who the other suspect was?"

"No, we're leaving that one up to you. We'll move in when you want us to. Just follow him when possible, note where he goes and who he meets. But always use the BAR code when updating us."

"I'll find out from chief Hermes who this guy is and where he's coming from," Joe said as though pinning him down was an easy procedure.

"No, for God's sake don't do that. The chief is okay in our books but for the secrecy needed here we have to keep this among ourselves," urged Johnson.

Kavinsky sat back a little when hearing this. "But I thought Hermes was all tuned in to this scenario by the DEA. I already discussed my role with him since you indicated it was okay to do."

"That's fine Joe. It's just that this has become so sensitive now that the fewer people knowing about these developments the better—the less there is to talk about this and spread it to others the less dangerous this becomes."

He added, "And don't forget, this isn't a fun group we're dealing with. It may very well even be tied in with Al-Qaida and Osama bin Laden."

"How do they get involved in this?"

"Mideast opium may be involved, Joe. As I said drugs and terrorism go hand-in-hand very often. And don't forget the Bahamas. The Bahama government once was accused of taking bribes from Colombian drug lords."

Upon departing to his police job again, Joe began wondering how safe this so-called secret operation really was for his wife—and perhaps even his uncle Al. After all, as a local police reporter his uncle was spotlighted in the press as having been helpful in implicating some previously-respected Twin Citians in a drug smuggling scandal connected with the Bahamas, Colombia and who knows where else—perhaps even among the Taliban.

Joe felt so concerned, in fact, that when getting into his squad car, he began dialing Al for some of his welcomed wisdom on behind-the-scene matters. Unlike Terry, he was completely sure that his uncle knew when to keep his mouth shut.

Since Al must been making his rounds on his reporting beat, Joe left a voice-mail message at his newspaper office saying simply: "Unc, gotta see you for lunch—very important. Will meet you at our favorite watering hole, Joe." He somewhat kept in mind Johnson's warning not to be specific, knowing that his reliable uncle would remember exactly when and where their "important" meetings take place.

CHAPTER 9

❀

Al Benjamin in the meantime was busy behind his word processor at the Tribune completing a story on a grocery store holdup in north Minneapolis.

But his reporter mind kept wandering back to his recent accidental encounter with his nephew at the mall. Al was indeed a snoop when it came to sniffing out anything that might make a story.

Why, he asked himself, was Joe in hot pursuit of a woman who might be fleeing from the law? What happened at the mall? and if this was just a shoplifter why was Joe so involved—why not just notify the store detective?

Al felt relieved upon getting the phone call from Joe. He hoped that some of these questions might be answered since for some reason he believed he was being put off about this. That's also why he immediately said yes to Joe's suggestion for a luncheon meeting the next day. He felt something was up, and wanted the low-down on what it was.

The fact that Joe mentioned their "favorite watering hole" as a meeting place meant that they should get together at the Cove Hideaway, which in turn indicated to Al that this would be a serious luncheon. Seems whenever they met at that rinky-dink eatery they talked "shop," including things that might be considered privileged information—just between cop and reporter. But the main reason was that it was so out of the main stream—away from the action—that they could quickly find a table far removed from the few patrons that drifted in. Moreover, although the service was fast the poor food helped keep crowds away as well as the often lukewarm beer.

Despite all these negatives, however, Al showed up ahead of time mostly to kid his nephew about always being late. He could get away with it easier before Joe got married, however, since he could always scold him about spending too much time with the chicks. Joe would always counter by calling his uncle a red-neck chauvinist.

Al smiled when recalling the many good times he's had with his favorite nephew, but quickly frowned when an overweight waiter with a cigar hanging from his mouth placed a rather stale beer on his table. He was somewhat startled and caught off guard when Kavinsky suddenly pulled up a chair and instantly put a finger against his lips as though getting ready to tell his uncle a secret.

"Don't say a word, unc. Just listen. I'll make this short and not so sweet. I hope you didn't mention our meeting to anyone, cause what I'm about to say is our secret and ours alone. Don't write anything down…just remember what's told you."

Al's mouth remained partially opened in surprise, even though he swallowed some of that gosh-awful brew while hearing Joe report on his mysterious activities during the past few days.

He knew his nephew experienced many tough and sensitive projects as a cop, but also knew when Joe acted this serious about something there should be warning flags all over the place.

"Be extremely careful uncle Al, and that goes for aunt Kay, make sure you notice anything out of the ordinary. These spooks we're dealing with come in a variety of shapes, sizes and disguises.

"Make a note of any callers, or even your sidekicks at work who may be acting strangely around you—like wanting to know where you've been, where you're going, or who your seeing."

"And for God's sake, don't mention you've been seeing me."

"How do I protect myself, Joey?" said his uncle rather nervously.

"By calling me on my cell phone—I'll even have it on in bed. Don't use my regular phone number. Also, I suggest just between you and me that you carry my little derringer that I used in the Bahamas, it got me out of lots of scrapes with those druggies over there, including Beck's thugs.

Passing the pistol under a napkin to Al, Kavinsky said "I already have a license to use it and I'll work on getting you one, in the meantime wear it and be sure it's loaded. Conceal it and don't tell anyone about it—or about our conversation."

"When did you say this drug lord's coming?" asked Al.

"I didn't. For all I know he may be here right now—hell he may be at the next table. But I doubt it, I'd know those cold eyes and expression anywhere. Guess that's why the DEA wants me on the case."

Getting up to leave, Al tugged Joe's arm teasingly, "tell me, did you ever catch up with your girl friend on the mall escalator?"

"She's much too fast for me," Joe chuckled. "Besides how do you know it was a girl?"

"You mean, it may have been a guy in a skirt?"

"Maybe…all I know is she, he or it certainly had great legs," joked Kavinsky recalling his futile chase.

He became quite serious, though, going out the door with Al.

"Remember now, unc, no stories in your newspaper on this, promise?"

He added, "however, you might just keep your eyes open for any suspicious behavior. Let me know right away if you come across anyone or anything that might be involved. Being a good newsman, you'll be able to sniff out a scoop—but tell it to me, not to your readers or any of your newspaper buddies."

With that in mind, and in full agreement, they left for their duties of the day headed in different directions.

When Joe returned to his precinct he dialed his cell phone for any messages, as he usually did during most of his assignments. He had only one call—from BAR. It was from Terry—he just said: "call me ASAP!"

When he reached Johnson, he was told: "He's here, Joe. My Guy and our other informants said Beck arrived in the U.S. this morning. Where or how we still don't know. But be on the lookout—we expect he'll be up our way soon."

Kavinsky hung up quickly and nervously, looking about as though he was being watched. "My God," he mumbled to himself, "this is starting to get to me—I'm becoming paranoid over all this."

To help escape this tension, Joe and Sarah visited Hennepin Avenue for some entertainment and great food that evening. His bride still worked casual hours at Nieman Marcus in downtown Mnneapolis and also enjoyed forgetting ahout work whenever possible and having fun in the big city. It would be wonderful both agreed if they could come up with enough money someday to have a more relaxed lifestyle.

"You dance divinely, my dear," said Joe as he swung Sarah around in step to a cool disco song. "You're not so bad yourself old man," she laughed snuggling up closer to Joe as the floor lights dimmed.

It was while they were twirling around that he spotted the rookie cop who sat down uninvited at his meeting with Paulson at the precinct lunchroom and interrupted their conversation. He still didn't recall the guy's name even though he met him only a few days ago, but did remember that he was the one whose saliva matched that of the photo-group suspect.

The rookie cop didn't notice Joe and Sarah, which is why Kavinsky seemed to accidentally nudge him while spinning Sarah near his table. The nudge was enough to almost knock the drink from his hands. Some spilled onto the sport coat of the new cop who looked up as though he was about to slug Kavinsky. But he stopped when he saw who bumped him.

"Oh, excuse me fella. I guess I got too infatuated with my partner," said Joe apologetically.

He looked at the young man and said "Hey, aren't you the one who joined us for lunch the other day at the police precinct?"

Surprised by his sudden recognition, the upset rookie cop stuttered somewhat before rising and extending his hand. "Yes—I remember, you're Mr. Kavinsky and your companion was Paulson—Dave Paulson".

Joe noted his accent—and formality—much unlike the typical all-American style. It sounded more Mid Eastern. In fact, as Joe began wondering about this fella, he thought his complexion was more brown than white.

"Yeah—but I'm sorry I seem to have forgotten your name," said Joe in his sneaky way trying to draw him out.

"Amad—Amad Turkos. I've been on the force only a short time, and am looking forward to working with you."

"I guess you have to get those orders from chief Hermes, Amad. Paulson is my partner now. I travel all around on a variety of assignments."

"Yes, that's what I've heard," responded Amad. Joe wasn't quite sure what he meant by this—and who may have talked about him to this newcomer.

"Oh, by the way lieutenant, this is my partner tonight," he said with a smile. He pointed to a young lady wearing a scarf over her head, Muslim style.

Joe couldn't help thinking no wonder she wasn't on the dance floor with Amad—she was lucky she didn't have to put a hood also over her eyes for him.

"Nice meeting you…have you two been taking in the sights of our fair city?" asked Joe to stall the meeting as Sarah began looking at her watch. He then introduced Sarah and asked, "have you been to our great mall yet or the IDS tower?"

Kavinsky was surprised, when Amad butted in before his date could speak and said sharply, "No, we really don't like those places. There's so many crowds and traffic."

Glad to bid this strange couple farewell, Joe looked at Amad and said simply, "Well, guess I'll be seeing you at work."

"They we're certainly different," remarked Sarah as she and Joe danced away to the other side of the hall where their table was located.

"Yeah—very," said Joe. "Just between you and me, I think I'll check them out some more. Who knows, that gal may have been the one I was running after at the mall."

Sarah didn't say a word about this until she got Joe home and they were ready for bed. "What do you mean you were chasing a woman around the mall?" she said rather teasingly with here hands on her hips in her sexy little nightie.

Joe blushed in defense, saying "I can't explain it yet, honey. Just believe me—it was strictly police matters."

They hardly began to get together under the covers when the phone interfered. Almost hesitant to answer for fear the DEA wanted him again for something, he was somewhat relieved when it turned out to be just uncle Al.

"Joey, I got a thought. Your aunt Kay and I would like you and Sarah over to our house tomorrow evening for dinner to discuss it. It's a good one Joe—you'll like it."

Although Joe could figure out the real purpose of the call was to talk about his "secret pursuit" for the lady on the escalator, he noticed his uncle was following instructions by not mentioning Beck or any specifics. And by keeping the call brief—it could be passed off by anyone listening as just a dinner invitation among friends.

'Thanks unc, count on us." Joe then hung up, knowing Al wouldn't be bothered by the short response. If anything, it might pique Al's interest, he shrugged.

Before dining with the Benjamins, however, Kavinsky had his work cut out for him the next day. While not dealing with regular police matters, he checked with the crime lab again just to make sure the Paulson sample wasn't the one that matched the person who held

Joe's coffee cup—and probably poured poison into it—while Joe was kind enough to take a picture of their group visiting the mall.

Recalling his "accidental" meeting with Amad, or whatever his real name might be, Joe began thinking about the many faces smiling at him when he snapped that Polaroid type shot of them. It was tough to identify any one of them, however. Seems all the men wore beards down to their necks and some had hair bands. Most of the women were covered in robes down to their feet.

This made him wonder all the more why Amad was clean shaven?

Maybe he wasn't in the group when someone told him to hold the cup...but on the other hand, thought Joe, the group was all by itself...away from everyone else. About all he knew for sure at this point was that Amad was the prime coffee-holding suspect and thanks to some ingenious DNA he now had the proof he needed.

Riding up to uncle Al's in their slightly new car, that was still decorated with some confetti letting everyone know it was used recently to convey newlyweds, Joe and Sarah were met at the door by a sweet, smiling middle-aged aunt Kay. She stood in front of a bald, smiling bespectacled guy with a pencil behind his ear. You could always tell Al was indeed a wordsmith, and proud of it.

"Boy, it you wanted to remain inconspicious, Joe, you might have tried to get all those decorations off your car," his uncle chuckled.

"I'm a very busy guy," Al, "but I knew I could count on my uncle to do this for me," Joe teased back.

Such kidding continued even around the dinner table as aunt Kay kept bringing in a tempting variety of great food. A little wine, and of course beer for Al, added to the lightness of the evening which was mixed with very little seriousness. The only real somber moments came when Kay and Sarah began taking the dishes into the kitchen and remained there chatting about women matters.

Knowing they now had a little time to talk turkey, instead of eating it, Joe and his uncle spoke softly about how the chase was going in catching Beck and his bad bunch. Al immediately focused on his "thoughts" relating to the whereabouts of Beck. Instead of going ahead with this, however, he began by first going backward.

"Tell me Joe, other than the great mall, where is the next—or perhaps first—place of prominence around this state?"

"What do I win if I guess it?" asked a quizzical, amused Kavinsky.

"Seriously, have you ever asked where would be the best place and strategy if you were Beck to stay unnoticed and secure if you wanted to come back to a country that's been trying for years to imprison you?"

"At one of our casinos?" Joe continued to joke.

"I'll give you a tip—especially after reading the paper today. This should make it easy for you. It's a very popular spot just a few miles south of here. One that's visited by distinguished, and not so distinguished, personalities from all around the world."

"Could its main attraction be healthcare—instead of black-jack?"

"You got it. The state's most famous clinic is often a gathering place for thousands of visitors probably every day, some of whom want to come undisclosed for one reason or another. For example, some who want extra secrecy and privacy about their health problems."

"And some use it as a sneaky way to enter the country and do evil?" responded Joe looking at his uncle to know if he's understanding all this.

"Exactly, Joe. You're ahead of me. If you read our other daily newspaper across the river, instead of that so-called newspaper you subscribe to, you'd also know why I'm bringing this up. In Sunday's issue it mentioned that a large group of international executives, about 25 of them, are flying to the clinic along with other 'comrades' having special medical needs."

"And they're coming, probably under pretense of getting physicals or obtaining more knowledge of what this great clinic offers, and they're from all over, Joe—the Mideast, Europe even Colombia and the Bahamas." Al looked at Joe to see what expression he'd get when the latter country was mentioned.

"The Bahamas—Bimini maybe?" was all Kavinsky could ask.

"Aha, now you're connecting, nephew. There was no specific mention of the places, but why not Bimini? After all, you indicated this may be a global gathering of the kingpins. And who could be more 'king-pinish' than Beck?"

"You're right again, unc. And Beck has a lot of stuff he's dealing with here, and back and forth."

"When are they arriving at the clinic unc?"

"Again nephew, if you would read that other newspaper, it speculated that all those sheiks and lords are scheduled in the next couple of weeks. All very kingly and respected, of course, but needing some medical attention.

"I wouldn't believe everything that rag of yours says," kidded Joe. "But it does make you wonder."

"It sure does, Joey. With just a little disguise, our friend Beck would be difficult to spot in that crowd."

"He'd be the one with the cigarette hanging from his lips."

"That's right, you've seen him up close haven't you."

"To an extent—you never want to get too close to that guy. He's an assassin many times over."

"Yeah—and I understand he has a real harem and henchmen at his command who'll do just about anything for him," added Al.

"Maybe, in fact, like bin Laden. Some who would jump through hoops and maybe even fly into buildings like they did at the World Trade Center."

As the evening wound down, and Kay and Sarah got involved in a game of exciting dominoes, the cop and reporter lightened up and began talking about catching Minnesota's favorite fish—the walleye—up north soon. For years Benjamin loaned out his cabin a few miles from the Canadian border to any of his nephews or nieces who wanted to get away from the pace of the big cities.

"You still got that toy motor on your boat?" teased Joe.

"Yeah, but I patched up the boat shed and did other repair work—you wouldn't recognize the old place. Even put a hammock on the porch. It's just waiting for you and Sarah to pay a visit," he said smiling at Joe's bride.

With that, Joe looked at his watch as though it was now time to go hit the "hammock" at home with Sarah. "I'm eager to take you up on that cabin invitation, unc. But right now I think I'll be doing some traveling south in the state instead of north."

He added, "In fact, I've been having some arthritis in my knee lately. Maybe I'll get a checkup at that clinic we're talking about so much." He waived to his uncle as he and Sarah headed out the door.

CHAPTER 10

The next day Joe was quick to notify Terry Johnson and Chief Hermes of his intended clinic trip. Both were quite agreeable, but Terry especially warned Joe of the danger he may be running into.

"You're probably being watched very closely by those paving the way for Beck. So try to confuse them with your moves. If you go there be sure to actually see a doctor. Don't fake anything—these guys are real pros when it comes to detecting anything suspicious. Also, if you have any DNA questions the docs there are the ones to quiz—they're such experts that I understand they expect to store patient DNAs even on a credit card-sized chip."

"I can alert the clinic police to keep an eye on you, too," added Hermes.

"No, don't do that chief!" interrupted Johnson. "We're not sure of anyone in this scenario. Who knows who Beck may have influenced down there with all his wealth—even the most loyal cop. This has to be our little secret...the protection comes from our DEA undercover. We'll have a couple of agents on hand when you get there, Joe. They'll get in touch with you in their own confidential way. Believe me, it will be safer that way."

Kavinsky shrugged, noting that he'll be sure to read more about the global executive clinic visit and to research it before heading down there. "Well, you better do it this weekend, cause what I know—that bunch will be arriving from all over the world this coming week."

Both at his precinct desk and near the fireplace of his home, the detective read and re-read every bit of news about the coming of the notable visitors. It certainly was pleasing to clinic officials, since, like so many dignitaries around the world most had their choice of going to any excellent medical clinic they considered best for their special problems. Apparently the Minnesota clinic headed the list.

Taking advantage of this upcoming event, of course, was the clinic's public relations department. But its satellite clinics in Arizona and Florida sort of shrugged it off since the main focus was on their headquarter facility. Joe learned some time ago not to expect much cooperation from that PR staff since it was almost traditional not to highlight anyone coming for exams or treatments due to its strict policy of patient privacy.

In fact, Kavinsky held back somewhat. Before delving into this anymore he briefed Terry about planning to remain in the background when the group lands near the clinic airport rather than making any big arrangements to talk to any of them or play any visible role that could tip off Beck—or alert or upset the PR guys there.

Johnson's reaction was cool. "Joe, you should have been exploring the procedures used to visit the clinic. The DEA knows that you just don't come there without first filling out a multi-page health questionaire, about a mile long. And once you're there, you usually have to get other things done before you even see a doctor."

"Like what?" asked the surprised Kavinsky.

"Like blood tests, etcetera, etcetera."

"So we got him," said Joe, jumping up from his chair like a kid catching a ball.

"Hold on—these guys have to agree to pre-exam entry tests."

"Yeah—and if one of them doesn't, he may be our suspect." reasoned the detective.

"They usually all do Joe. There's no way you're going to beat the system down there."

Kavinsky got up, lit a cigarette, and blew the smoke toward the ceiling as though deep in thought. He finally said, "the DNA—the DNA man. That's what the DNA is all about."

"What are you smoking Joe? Whatever it is you better stop or we'll put the cuffs on you," responded Terry grinning.

"Don't you get it Terry? If everyone gets his blood taken then we'll really know which one is Beck?"

Johnson didn't say a thing. He just looked intently at Joe and nodded his head as if in agreement. "You've got something there. But there's one big problem—we've got to have a match."

This caused a pause in the conversation. But after quickly mulling this over, Joe snapped his fingers and said, "How about causing our leading suspect to bleed—maybe by an accident. With the blood we get, we can bring it to the lab in a hurry to catch him."

"Are you nuts? Do you think we should stab each one?" mocked Johnson. "Settle down Kavinsky. Right now we should try to get as organized as possible—no blood shed. Well...maybe just a little scratch or so," Terry allowed.

Becoming serious, Johnson then informed Joe that all the appropriate clinic doctors have already been advised to make certain the blood work is done first—without indicating anything suspicious. "Remember, this is all routine as far as they're concerned."

"As for the scratch?" Joe asked, determined to find out why Johnson even mentioned it. "Quite simple, If your suspect goes along with all this pre-entry blood work it may pay us to set up a situation where he might be more likely to accidentally cut himself on something."

"What then?"

"Then we can trace the tiny blood stain to the visitor who has the same match that the clinic has—and that's our man."

CHAPTER 11

❁

"But there's some more things that puzzle me Terry," Joe added. "How and when do we know Beck's schedule and how can we possibly set up a plan to scratch him for blood?"

Johnson sat down on the chair next to the door, drew a deep breath, excelled and frowned at Joe. He appeared annoyed, as though being interrupted in his plan to leave, but determined to make sure Kavinsky understood what's going on.

"Joe—you're forgetting our ace in the hole. Remember My Guy? He's with Beck right now. Don't worry you'll have a suspect to try this on—just follow My Guy's directions when he contacts you. Also, Beck's not going to get his checkup appointment if he doesn't follow the steps for checking in."

"By the way, instead of BAR, his call letters will be *MG*. When you hear that you'll know it's him," advised Johnson.

"Sounds like a fancy car dealer trying to sell me new wheels."

"That's okay—the more we can throw Beck's gang off the better it is for all of us."

At this, Terry slipped Joe a note under the table, as though cameras may be on them. It read: "to get in touch with My Guy" and listed phone numbers to call.

As Terry rose to leave, he looked sternly at Kavinsky saying, "and Joe forget about being there when he arrives. They know you—don't forget they masterminded a plan to get you at the mall. They'll be on the lookout for you. You won't last very long down there. They may attack you again—to scare you off, or worse."

"Then who do you suggest to be my backup? You know I can spot Beck best having seen him. And no other cop, at least none that's still alive, can say that."

"How about your uncle? He's no cop."

Joe almost fell back onto his chair when hearing this. How would Johnson even know he had been talking with Al?

"Why not?—he's a newspaperman, and a good one at that. He'd fit right in with the many other media having legitimate reasons for a story and photos on the group's arrival," explained Terry. "Let's say, he'll be a lot less conspicuous than you, and can be another excellent source in keeping us informed."

Kavinsky hesitated, mostly because he didn't want his uncle in harm's way. Before he could comment, however, Terry added, "what the hell, Joe, knowing the close relationship you two have with one another I'm pretty sure you've already brought him into this one way or the other."

About all Joe could do was shrug. He put out his cigarette and hoped his body language would indicate he wasn't too excited about the plan.

Kavinsky had regained his composure when approaching Al at the newspaper office the next day. He wasn't quite sure, however, how his uncle would react when included in this unusual spying scenario.

"Hi unc, thought I'd catch you for a cup of coffee before you run off on your news beat. How you been feeling after all that trauma you went through in running down those druggies?" Joe said for openers. He knew Al was on medicine for his shoulder pain when he encountered some of Joe's drug suspects in the past.

"Joey—what a nice surprise seeing you here—usually we connect by telephone or e-mail."

He added, "as for how I'm feeling—not so hot. My joints are still bothering me a lot. In fact, your aunt Kay and I talked about it the other day and we think it's best that I visit the clinic one of these days to get a second opinion."

This gave Kavinsky an opener to talk about the clinic project, but he knew he had to get his uncle in a secluded spot to go into the secret details.

Al's suggestion to meet at a Timberwolves basketball game seemed absurd to Joe at first. But with the Wolves popularity on the downswing and plenty of empty seats near the top rafters, they both could hear one another clearly while away from most of the rather indifferent spectators. Plus, it gave Al another chance to howl like a wolf, as most of the Wolves' fans do occasionally for their underdog hometown team.

It didn't take Joe long sitting on the uncomfortable upper level seats to convey to his uncle what Beck was all about and how important it was to track him down. He agreed with his uncle that both good and evil folks head for the mammoth Minnesota clinic if they think they have a major health problem. "I guess they all want to live forever—at least 'till everyone is under their control," Joe theorized.

Nodding to all this, Al told Joe that he could get a real good handle on what makes Beck tick from the stories that appeared years ago in the newspapers. His paper, the Trib, had a large "morgue" of stories and pictures on file and he would rummage through that when he got back to the office. He already knew that Beck originated from the Midwest and went to convent schools. He apparently began as a wholesome lad before getting hooked on cocaine.

CHAPTER 12

In addition to scouring the old newspaper files, Benjamin also wanted an overview of what other publications were also saying about Beck and his criminal ways. For this reason, he also visited some libraries to get as much news as possible about this international drug baron.

His search went back about 20 years when Robert J. Beck was a respectful businessman, husband and father. He came from a rather humble family, carrying papers in grade school, mowing lawns during high school and branching out doing various odd jobs to get through college—a small christian school near the outskirts of Cleveland. He majored in economics and received high marks in math, his old records showed, which could account for some of his clever ways of making money.

During Al's research, he also discovered that Beck married his high school sweetheart and was resigned to living a quiet suburban life around his home town for a long time. All the while, however, he found a way to deceive his wife and family by hooking up with a dope smuggling ring. One day he kissed his wife on his way to work and never came back. He then completely disappeared, much to the dismay of police and federal agents who later discovered he was controlling a drug trafficking business.

You might say Al looked at all sides of this guy and all the pictures he could find, from his time of child innocence to when he turned into a monster—quick to get rid of anyone in his way. Police around the world could never pin him down. They knew he spent time in the Bahamas but, like bin Laden, he was always too clever to get cornered.

As Joe emphasized to his uncle, the only thing you can be sure of about Beck are his glaring green eyes, slim face, long nose and scowl around his mouth. Most of this could be covered by a beard, of course, but not the icy stare of his beady eyes, once they hook on to you or suspect you of disloyalty. If you get this stare, remember it—and watch your back! cautioned Joe.

Al kept researching Beck and his whereabouts while preparing to be among the press on hand for the arrival of the clinic's very prestigious guests, Kavinsky resumed keeping a close eye on Amad, the rookie precinct cop. Joe still hoped this might possibly lead to seeing the young hooded lady again who asked him to snap her sinister group's picture at the mall.

Stalking one of the precinct's own cops may be a bit complex, thought Joe, even if he was just out of the police academy. That's why Joe contacted Johnson and with his okay paid a call on chief Hermes to brief him about this.

The smile on Hermes' face when Joe entered the chief's office changed quickly to a frown when he heard of Joe's suspicions regarding Amad. "Going after one of our own guys Joe? This sounds a bit weird. But it's okay with me as long as you got approval from the DEA. There must be records on Amad and you're also free to check his personnel files here. I'll make sure only you, the DEA and myself know about this."

Kavinsky not only went through the files, but also managed to schedule the same coffee breaks and meals as Amad. He didn't want to be too noticeable, however, so he mostly did his observation while strolling by Amad's desk or trying to hear some of the conversation he had with his fellow cops.

He especially noticed a very pretty young lady who visited with Amad one day—for some reason Joe felt he knew her from somewhere. He was so far away, however, that she couldn't see him.

While working late one afternoon, he also noticed Amad was still on the phone talking very seriously. The clock showed that Joe would be late for Sarah's fine cooking so he called her to let her know to go ahead and eat without him. He got her voice-mail and was informed that Sarah also was running late with some of the neighborhood women holding a baby shower next door. Joe no sooner got his message completed when Amad got up from his chair, looked all around as if trying to find someone, and hurried out of the precinct station and into its parking lot.

Kavinsky had a hunch that Amad was on a mission. He waited until Amad got into his car and, with daylight fading, tried tailing him—making sure he was always about several cars behind to avoid any suspicion by Amad that he was being followed.

Joe had to squint at times from the sharp glare of the setting sun through his car window to see the quick turns Amad made and to press hard on the accelerator when Amad got onto the straight-aways. It was as though the pursued also wasn't sure where the hell he was going.

About five miles off the freeway, in a rather isolated suburb, Joe noticed that Amad suddenly pulled up next to a home in the middle of similar very low-income housing in that neighborhood. He couldn't help but think out loud, "Lord, he should be able to afford better than this—even on a rookie's salary."

Kavinsky parked several blocks away, turned off his lights and watched Amad walk up to the front door. Although he couldn't hear what was said, it was obvious that the person opening the door was a woman with a hood who was quite pleased to greet him. Whoever it was, gave him a big hug and a very long and passionate kiss.

Realizing there wasn't much to do than sit in his car for who knows how long, Kavinsky dialed his wife from his cell phone. Still getting no response, he began leaving another voice-mail: "I might be a little later than I thought honey…I'm still on assignment. Can't tell you anymore, other than I'm safe and…"

But before he could finish, Sarah cut in. "Joe—I just got home, too. I don't know where you are…but if it's of any importance, some man with a strange voice called a second or two ago to find out if you were here."

"What's his name?"

"I don't know, he just mumbled it as though he didn't want to let me know. The Caller-ID came up with 'unavailable.' I thought it was another telemarketing guy, but he asked where you might be reached and when you'll get back."

"What did you tell him?"

"I said I don't know to both—where are you anyway?"

"I'll tell you later. I should be home soon…keep that beer cold. Love you—but gotta go now." His abrupt rush to click off his call to Sarah was prompted when he noticed more lights turning on in the home that Amad entered. Could it be that Amad's secret lover was that mysterious young woman at the mall?

He also thought perhaps Amad may have noticed Joe's car tailing him. After all, eluding and following cars was a basic class even for rookies.

With that in mind, Kavinsky turned off his headlights several blocks away, put his collar up, and began strolling casually along the dark block where Amad and the others in the house were parked. Joe pretended as though he was just a neighbor out for a stroll. He brought along his note book and pen light which he blinked on quickly whenever he spotted a license-plate to check our the numbers.

Joe didn't wait for the "party" to break up, however, he wanted to get the hell out of that area as fast as possible. It wasn't until mid morning of the following day that he had any time away from his regular police duties to search for the names of the owners of the license numbers he wrote down.

To his surprise, however, they all belonged to authorized and legitimate Minnesota car drivers. Studying the computer printout once more, he began to wonder if his suspicions about Amad were merely imaginary. If they weren't, then a lot of guys driving around the Twin Cities were fooling the state's motor vehicle license department cause how could Amad qualify for an authorized driver's license.

Shrugging his shoulders as if dismissing the whole project, Kavinsky turned off the computer and put his file away on Amad, making sure it was under lock and key. In fact, he never batted an eye when bumping into Amad again at lunch. As Joe passed by, Amad smiled and raised his coffee cup in greeting while munching on a hamburger.

In the meantime, Al Benjamin was continuing his probe into the upcoming gathering of the so-called dignitaries at the clinic.

Since his newspaper was obviously, and embarrassingly, scooped by the competitor, the St. Paul Press, he had to review the files of "that other" newspaper on any story relating to the reported arrival and other details of the group. However, even reading all this didn't answer many of the questions Benjamin was looking for.

He figured the only way to find out more would be to "lower" himself to having lunch with his chief opponent at the Press—reporter Don Smiley—who apparently must have had some inside information about the coming of this strange group to out-scoop all the other newspaper reporters around Minnesota.

Although knowing his editor had strict rules about fraternizing with anyone from the competing paper, Al sneaked out from his cubicle shortly before noon the next day in hope of finding Smiley at his usual "drinking hole" in a little pub and restaurant near downtown St. Paul.

He lucked out. As expected, Smiley was all alone in a dark corner of the restaurant reading a newspaper while washing down a sandwich with a glass of beer. Al was surprised and somewhat disappointed, however, that Don was imbibing. He was known to be an alcoholic.

"Catching up on all the news from the Trib again Don?" said Al jokingly.

"What the hell brings you here?" Smiley responded. "Geez, if your boss knows you're mingling with the enemy you'll be shot."

"Just thought I'd check up on you. Haven't seen you around much lately. Usually we're bumping into one another on the same beats."

Smiley quit smiling when he heard this. "I haven't been feeling all that great lately Al."

"What's up, I see your byline all over your paper. You can't be too sick."

"I'm hoping so. But to make sure, I've been going to the clinic for some checkups."

Seeing his opening, Al quickly asked: "You and a lot of others I hear. Is that how you got the news on the coming of those big shots from around the world looking for special medical attention at the clinic?"

This made Smiley chuckle knowing his conquest over his fellow news hounds. "That was a real coup wasn't it Al. When you're lying down ready to be put through an MRI tube, you can easily hear the docs and nurses prepping you. Believe me, they're real excited down there with the coming of that crowd of Mideast big shots."

"Gosh Don, I hope you're feeling better. Your hearing must be really good though—to get all those details you included in your story."

"Naw—it's fading fast like I am," shrugged Smiley. "I just mentioned to the clinic PR guy before I left that it's certainly one more tribute to that place, and he then figured I knew all about the situation and answered all my questions."

"But you didn't say exactly when that bunch is coming. Doesn't anyone know down there?"

With that Smiley quit smiling again. "You ain't trying to scoop me are you snoop? If you were feeling as weak as I was at the time it was all I could do to remember what that PR hack was saying. I didn't even have a pencil with me. As I said, if it wasn't for that guy Sam Stone I would have had almost nothing to report. And I'm sure I wouldn't even have heard about it if I wasn't going through that MRI test."

Al picked up on the name Sam. This could at least give him a good start on getting more details from the clinic that Joe may want. But he felt dropping the subject was a good time, and began talking about other less newsy matters such as the Twins controversial baseball stadium and the Vikings' few victories. Al joined Smiley by ordering a beer.

In fact, Al took advantage of Smiley's alcoholic condition, and bought him a few more rounds while taking a few more drinks himself. As Smiley became more talkative, he offered some additional information about the upcoming clinic meeting with what he called the "clan."

"I don't know zactly when it's going to be, but I bet sometime late next week. The PR guy indicated the airline schedules for most are due by noon on Friday or so. They're coming from all directions, Al—East, West—God knows where else. I guess there's lots of sick kings and queens in that bunch. That damn PR guy knows everything—but won't talk much to us scoops-er, snoops."

As Smiley began to slur his words, Benjamin began feeling guilty taking advantage of a fellow reporter with a snoot full and nodded to a waitress standing by to bring his friend some black coffee. Letting Smiley know he had to be back on his beat, Al made a beeline to his auto cell phone to pass some of this information on to his nephew cop.

"Looks like I'll be taking my trip this week," Al said beginning his phone conversation with Joe, making sure no one tapping in could determine where he was heading.

"Sounds great, see you for lunch—same place same time. Bye," was all his nephew replied, knowing his uncle was on the same wave length and following the prescribed DEA phone security system.

Instead of lunch, both got together at Al's house for dinner to further confuse anyone on their trail. Aunt Kay whipped up her great fish dish again and then remained in the kitchen as Joe and Al talked turkey. She knew something very important was being discussed but was afraid to know what, considering the serious looks on their faces and the risky kind of work they get involved with from time to time.

This time the talk was all about Beck—how to get him.

"The DEA is helping to figure this out, but we probably have more of a chance than anyone," predicted Kavinsky. "If you and I can both be there when he arrives one of us will be able to detect who and where he is."

"Yeah, but he can probably decide where we are, too, and get us first," warned Al. "Look what he's done so far. He almost killed you Joey with poison at the mall. They got their eye on you…none probably know or care about me."

"Don't be so sure, unc. You've been connected with me during our drug roundup a few months ago—and wrote some headline stories about this. But you're right, they probably won't spot you right away in a crowd—and they may me, especially if one of my own precinct cops is part of their group," theorized Joe, recalling his suspicions about Amad. He then quietly told Al about his photo-shoot incident at the mall and how he almost caught the cloaked person arranging this.

Agreeing to a plan that would involve Joe tipping off Terry Johnson first and then having Al go to the clinic to get more facts from the clinic's PR man, Joe left his uncle with the request that he let him know when the best time would be to also be at the clinic to help nab Beck.

Upon returning home and hugging his bride real hard, the cop saw a message on his phone. He clicked onto it. Aunt Kay's voice said simply: "9 a.m. Saturday."

Like his nephew, Benjamin put shopping far down on his "fun list." This was why he was so disgruntled when his wife asked him to go with her to the mall for a special sale that evening. It was more difficult for him to say no than to go along, so he opted for the latter and found himself sitting on a bench where other grumpy old men were resting waiting for their spouses to finish rummaging through the sales merchandise.

Just by coincidence, his nephew was also encouraged by his wife to attend the super sale. Seems Sarah heard about this special event when talking with Kay and phoned her husband at work. As Joe was trying unsuccessfully to weasel out of this, he heard a click on his phone as though someone else was tapping in. He immediately hung up and checked his caller-ID, but nothing came up. On the way out of the precinct he noticed most of his fellow workers already had gone. Only Amad was still at his desk. He looked up and smiled as Joe passed by.

That smile, thought Joe, looked vaguely familiar. But all of those guys posing for him at the mall had long beards and it was tough to identify any one face. But still, he pondered, that expression on Amad's face seemed to ring a bell for some reason.

Before taking off again for the mall, Joe, as planned, contacted Johnson at DEA, using the code name TJ, and briefed him on the latest information he obtained, including from his uncle. Terry liked the fact that Benjamin was researching this and got some special info from those very close to the source regarding Beck's coming.

"We'll also have our people in the welcoming crowd and even with the press, Joe. If you think you see our man, we'll move in. We haven't heard from My Guy lately, but expect to very soon. Imagine he's pretty busy nosing around Beck who has a history of changing his mind often."

"Keep in mind he's to tell us what disguise Beck will be in and I'll be sure to pass this on to you as soon as I hear."

"Okay, but if it takes very long I'll plan to be at the clinic a couple of days before Friday. You have my cell phone number Terry. I'll be staying at the Koehler hotel.

"Sounds good. Over and out JOKE," acknowledged the DEA agent laughing at Joe's code name. "And in the meantime, keep watching your back old buddy."

CHAPTER 13

❀

Keeping his promise to go shopping, Joe tagged along with his pretty bride. He was somewhat relieved, however, to know Sarah preferred to go through the west entrance of the mall which opened close to Camp Goofy rather than through the extensive women's shoe department which he knew could capture Sarah's attention for hours.

Th west entrance also was the noisiest and had even larger barricades in front of it than the one Joe and Sarah walked through the last time they went mall roaming. It was so loud that morning, with all the kids yelling on the roller coasters and other fun rides, that Kavinsky became somewhat disoriented.

Encountering his uncle and aunt in this screaming mob would be impossible if it wasn't for the help of his cell phone. Good thing he had Al's private number.

"Where the hell are you unc?" Kavinsky asked loudly into his tiny phone.

"On the top floor. Kay saw some eye-glasses she wants to try on. Can't say when we'll be finished—although I'm about finished right now."

Kavinsky chuckled, appreciating what his uncle was saying. "Yeah, know what you mean. But hang in there—we'll be coming up to meet you soon as Sarah is through gazing around at everything. What store are you in?"

Before Joe could get an answer, however, his phone began beeping with the monitor flashing "TJ". Joe sensed it must be important and clicked into the call, putting Al on hold.

"Joe, I can't talk much. You may be in danger—we all might. Just got word that My Guy has been kidnapped—he's been taken somewhere. When and where I don't know yet, our Bahama agent just notified us. Apparently Beck is on to us—his gang may know about you. They may be torturing My Guy for all we know. Continue with your plans, but stay alert and keep me posted if anything interrupts your traveling plans."

Kavinsky could hardly believe what he was hearing. The main informant for the DEA was gone...the closest contact to get that bastard Beck.

Joe tried calling Al back, but apparently his uncle was also on the phone.

Sarah began tugging on his arm to come see a colorful and very brief swim suit ideal for sun tanning—and catching the eyes of every man on the beach.

While Sarah was describing this attractive swimwear, Joe could only think of one thing. Although Sarah would be disappointed, he had to let his uncle know immediately of the possible danger that could be lurking about for anyone involved with getting Beck.

Since he couldn't contact Al by phone, Joe told Sarah he had to rush to the men's room and would be right back. He then ran up the escalators to the third level of the huge mall leaving Sarah wondering if his bladder was ready to explode, and if he was in such a hurry why he didn't simply run to the large restroom on the nearby first floor.

Joe wasn't sure where Al was, but he knew if his aunt was checking out glasses it could very well be at Eye Pleasure, the big optical store several yards away from where the escalator stops.

Sure enough, there was uncle Al—standing out in front of the store still looking at his cell phone, probably wondering what the hell happened to his nephew. He was surprised when Joe tapped him on the shoulder. But he became more than startled when he heard the news about My Guy.

"I warned you Joe, this is much bigger than the both of us. This is another bin Laden situation. If the feds can't get him, how the heck can we?"

He continued, "But I still want to know who my reporter pal Smiley was talking to at the clinic and find out more details. And I'm glad to know the feds will be around to keep an eye on us."

"Yeah—keep going with our plans unc. The DEA knows what we're doing and maybe they'll even find their 'my guy' by the time we're down there. The only thing I must warn you about again is to be sure not to let anyone know about this because if…

Kavinsky suddenly stopped talking—and almost held his breath, causing his uncle to ask "what's wrong Joey…you look like you've seen a ghost."

"Maybe I'm not seeing one, but I'm hearing about one," Joe said seriously.

"Listen to the piano music unc."

"My god, we haven't got time to be listening to music nephew, especially any that's so out of season," Benjamin shrugged with a grin.

"This one we sure do," declared Joe as he put down his phone and began humming to the tune—"You Better Watch Out…Santa's Coming to Town."

"That's our tip, Al, my buddy Pete the piano player downstairs must have seen that Muslim gal again entering the mall. She's probably down around his piano near the shoe department on the first floor.

"Gotta go unc and try to nab her. I'm going down the escalators I just came up on—you stay here and I'll let you know if she's coming your way. I'm sort of Santa's little helper now."

"But how do I recognize her?", asked Al

CHAPTER 14

❀

"You probably can't—but just be on the lookout for a gal in her twenties, half hidden in a burqa but exposed enough to let you know she's gorgeous under all that wrapping and still very shapely despite all of it around her."

"For God's sake, Joe, that isn't much to go on."

"If her mouth isn't covered unc, look for a smile that will knock your socks off," said Joe as he scampered away for the descending escalator."Just stall her—give me enough time to cuff her. Use any excuse to delay her," he almost hollered heading down to the first floor and the piano player.

Kavinsky knew he was getting close to the piano as its music became louder. But he wasn't sure when he got to the first floor if he would encounter just the girl with the burqa or also his rookie suspect Amad. He was getting the signal that Amad was on his trail as much as Joe was on his. After all, Kavinsky reasoned, it could well have been Amad who knew when and where Joe and Sarah were strolling on their previous visit to the mall…and the time for them to be approached for their cup of poison.

Almost leaping off the last couple of escalator steps, Kavinsky in his rush landed near the piano. His friend Pete was still playing the Santa song, while passersby kept smirking and smiling over the out-of-season tune. Pete looked up from the keys a bit startled upon seeing his cop friend.

"Where—where did you see her?" asked Joe almost out-of-breath.

"Hey Joe, boy—yeah. She just went by here a few minutes ago. Headed toward Goofy Land."

"Did she go in there, or continue on to the main shopping areas?"

"It was hard for me to keep an eye on her—but I know she didn't keep going straight. When she got to the entertainment section, though, I couldn't turn my head enough to be sure she went in there. You know, playing the piano keys and moving your head around doesn't go together very well, Joe. I only know she looked pretty much like your sketch, despite her partial face-scarf."

"You did great," said Joe patting Pete's shoulder. "I'm going to guess she's looking at, or already is on, one of those crazy rides at Goofy secretly talking murder with some of her crazy group. Just so she's not loaded with suicide bombs."

"Joe, don't you think you should have some backup?" asked the worried pianist.

"I've got my cell phone and some handcuffs, that's all I need. If necessary, I'll call store security to help me. But let me know if you see her again Pete just in case she gets by me."

"I'll play that darn tune again," promised Pete, "or tackle her as she runs around my piano."

"No, I think this time we should leave old Santa in the North Pole," Joe wisecracked.

Kavinsky ran off after suggesting that Pete return to playing his normal type music, mostly the soothing, romantic stuff that turns shoppers on to the perfume or lingerie departments. While heading for the entertainment center he contacted Al on his cell phone and told him to stay close to the escalators to spot the suspect and phone mall security if necessary for backup help.

Unfortunately, it was kids' day at the entertainment center, and it seemed everyone from 2—10 was jammed up near the entrance waiting to get an early start to take in all the events. It was obvious that one of the biggest, in both size and hilarity, was the ax-shaped twirly-bird ride that left you flying mostly upside-down.

But Joe figured his suspect wouldn't be on such a breath-taking thrill ride, nor the one that seemed to almost throw you out over a big section of the mall on a swing. Besides, it would be tough to talk to anyone on those with all the screaming.

He nearly got a neck pain looking around to see anyone clad in a burqa. It wasn't until he was ready to give up that he finally spotted two suspicious adults together at the very far end of the center. Not having binoculars, Kavinsky pushed through the crowd to get somewhat close to this couple. To avoid not being seen, he purposely strolled behind the tallest shoppers holding their kids.

However, he was sure that by the time he got to where he wanted to go his suspects would be gone since everyone seemed to be blocking his way, in a big rush to take in all the various exciting sights of the mall fun park.

Kavinsky stopped far enough away to get a fairly good view of the couple he thought looked familiar. They suddenly stopped, both talking and moving their hands as though they were mad at somethng or someone.

Joe had to squint a little to see if he could identify them. When they turned toward him, he ducked but still could make out their faces. The woman had removed the covering on her face and was indeed the one who stopped Joe for her group photo. The man was the big surprise. It was him!—it was Amad.

Kavinsky resisted the urge to arrest them both, knowing that he shouldn't blow his cover until checking with Terry Johnson. Instead, he put his hand over his cell phone, and talked very quietly to Terry hoping he could be heard despite the yelling of the many excited kids around him.

"Please—don't approach them," advised Johnson. "Leave them alone Joe. Let Amad be your road map to getting the one we mostly want—Beck. We no longer seem to have the help of My Guy. Who knows where he is. As for the girl, let her be too. We have to continue to let them think they're getting away with their sneaky plans. When they're down at the clinic we'll round them all up Joe."

"You mean follow her around when she leaves him here?"

"Yeah—and stay with her when she's all alone. When she leaves, stop her car as though she's speeding just to get her license information. You'll know more about her that way. But it's most important that no one in her bunch notice that she's being arrested. Call off mall security—do it with as much finesse as possible."

Johnson added sternly, "No way do we want to let Amad know we're on to him. He can lead us to where we should go. And be sure to tell your uncle, the news man, that the DEA and police don't want any mention in the press at this time about the suspects. We sure don't want the civil liberty crowd down on us."

"Gottcha," replied Kavinsky. "I'm still real surprised how Amad could have fooled me with that phony beard at the photo shoot. But it'll be tough controlling my uncle from getting a scoop, Terry. I'm sure he'll listen to reason, however, especially in catching that weasel Beck As for the gal, I'm not sure it's a good idea for me to be the arresting officer—she knows me, remember?"

"Right—get one of your uniform officers to do that. I'm sure you know best how to do this and who you can rely on. Use your phone—tell the officer to meet you somewhere when she leaves and stop her on the freeway, okay?"

"Sounds workable," Joe said. "Gotta go now and get that policeman. Will keep you posted Terry."

"Incidentally," added Joe before clicking off, "I'm also wondering what information you came up with regarding those license numbers I obtained at Amad's meeting place the other night. Who were those guys with him anyway?"

"Don't worry Joe, we're working on it."

With that Kavinsky made a call to chief Hermes and was told he would arrange with the nearby mall police precinct to have a traffic cop near the mall meet Joe at Camp Goofy in a few minutes.

"Tell him I'll be at the Goofy statue at the entrance to the entertainment center chief. But if our suspect isn't a licensed driver we'll have to figure another way to get information on her," Joe advised.

Although it seemed like a long wait for the uniformed traffic cop to show up, Kavinsky was pleased to know there was still time for their plan. Amad and his girl friend remained in some sort of serious discussion near the corner of the center.

After explaining the plan, Joe and the traffic officer followed the couple around until the hooded female left through one of the doors leading to the parking area. Luckily, she was alone when getting into an old coupe...which most likely didn't have seat belts.

When she drove off, the uniformed policeman was already at the level where her car would pass. He stepped out in front of the car, waiving his hands for her to stop. He still wore his traffic guard jacket so she knew he was a legitimate mall cop. Startled, she stamped on the brakes, nearly hitting him as she came almost to a screeching halt.

"'Excuse me miss" said the young officer. "But you went through a cross walk at high speed. I also notice you don't have your seat belts on."

"I don't have any," she said removing her head-dress entirely to speak to the officer. Her beautiful face nearly shocked the cop, especially when she smiled at him. This also made it more difficult for the officer to take out his ticket pad.

"I'm sorry miss, but you were going too fast and there is a state law now that you have to use seat belts."

Her smile vanished quickly as he asked for her driver's license. She hesitated at first, but then removed it from her purse impatiently and seemingly annoyed. The officer also went to the back of the car and checked her license plate numbers while making a note of her name and other ID information on her driver's license.

She embarrassed the young officer somewhat by fluttering her eye lashes at him when he got back to her. With a somewhat beckoning smile, she placed her hand on his when he returned her driver's license. In fact, he couldn't help but blush.

"I'll let you go this time lady, but you've got to be careful driving around here. There's thousands of folks coming and going from these parking lots."

Both the officer and Joe felt they came through okay with their little act. It would be hard for her to declare any police profiling. Hopefully, they got what they were after, and Joe would soon know more about this mysterious woman.

CHAPTER 15

After being informed to stop his pursuit by Joe, Al begrudgingly joined his wife shopping and later made plans to travel to the clinic to meet Sam, the clinic's PR man. Al figured if Sam tipped off Smiley of the Press more than two weeks ago about that upcoming foreign dignitary gathering, he should have more details now.

Realizing meeting with a public relations director at such a renowned medical center, with so many restrictions regarding press relations, would take some doing, Al promptly arranged for his routine medical checkup at the clinic. He let Sam know by phone that he would be there on personal health matters and wondered if he could do a nice promotional-type story about the clinic at that time.

The PR guy seemed pleased over the interest that Al's newspaper, with a much larger circulation than Smiley's, was showing in the clinic and the foreseeable great PR benefits. He was very agreeable when Benjamin asked if he could sit down with him at lunch. Although Al didn't mention it, he knew this was also the day before the Beck group was due to arrive.

Like a well-oiled machine, Al's checkup involving an X-ray of his arthritic shoulder, went fast. His files were in order and even many of the nurses around the department knew the good-natured newspaperman and helped to expedite his visit. He was already checked into his hotel, so it was just a matter of calling Sam to let him know he'd be seeing him at the Koehler restaurant at noon.

The cell phone on the belt around Benjamin's portly stomach, however, beat Al's attempt to make the call to Sam. It emitted a cute but loud tune alerting Al that he was being summoned by his nephew. "He Joey, what's up? I'm just about to put some final touches on preparing for the arrival of your weirdos." There was a pause that surprised Al, since usually his nephew would quickly have a clever response.

Instead, he heard: "Al—be extremely careful down there. This is really getting to be big and terrifying. The DEA has just informed me that their undercover, My Guy, has been murdered. He was decapitated and discovered all over the Bahamas. Someone must have guessed he was a spy in Beck's army."

All Al could say was "wow!" After regaining some composure, he added, "I wonder if this effects my interview with the PR director in any way."

"It shouldn't—I doubt if the government wants this known yet.

Just remember to confirm with your PR man that each arrival is treated as every patient is entering the clinic—getting their blood and other health records checked as part of the required visit there. Johnson told me that My Guy, before his death, was able to send him a sample of Beck's blood without his knowing it. Seems My Guy had a way to collect blood and saliva from Beck's toothbrush."

"Geez, I hope that didn't cause My Guy's death."

"Yeah, they sure seem to know exactly what we're up to."

The luncheon meeting with the clinic PR director went well. In fact, thought Al, it seemed Sam went along with everything mentioned. Being an experienced interviewer, Al knew all the questions to ask to make the PR guy think the clinic was about to be given super space in the newspaper citing how wonderful it is. Sam was proud to mention that the skyscraper clinic is visible for ten miles across rolling meadows and cornfields, and that its reputation hosts over a million patients a year and has so many visitors from foreign nations that it has translators for more than 30 languages.

Looking around at the ritzy place they were eating in, Al was reminded by its glitter that the entire medical complex reflected the outstanding image of this internationally famed health center. Too bad, he thought, that the spectacular goodness of this immense health center might soon be mired in ugly evil.

Al approached the subject matter very carefully and at just the proper time. After hearing the PR director boast about the many different patients attracted to the clinic, also regarded as the "motherhouse" for all its satellites around the nation, the reporter regarded this as the time to do more snooping. He used an indirect approach. "Yeah, it's sure one heck of a great place you've got here Sam. Everyone thinks of it when wanting the ultimate in care. Also, I understand the great leaders around the world are even in awe of the progress your researchers have made to combat even the most severe special health problems."

This led Sam to interrupt and almost arrogantly add, "You're so right Al." He then looked about—as though someone might be listening—and whispered in Al's ear. "I'll let you in on something else…we expect some of the greatest leaders to be arriving tomorrow."

Al made sure he looked surprised and awaited more news. He then leaned over to hear Sam continue with what he thought was another great tribute to the clinic.

"They'll be here around 10:15 and be led into our back entrance. They seem to be very humble and certainly don't want any fanfare. They all have special problems and look to us to help them. We're quite honored that they chose us Al—you might add that to your story on our being recognized as a top medical mecca," Sam beamed, as though seeing the great feature article being developed and the appreciation bestowed on him by his bosses for making this happen.

"But will they be treated like everyone else? Everyone gets an equal chance at being helped, right?" asked Al leading the PR guy on.

"Exactly, they'll all undergo entrance checkups and be assigned to our top docs."

"So, what you're saying is they'll have to undergo everything we do—filling out papers, getting blood work, being weighed in, and all those things before their detailed personal health consultations?"

Stone considered this for a moment. "Perhaps not so much paper work—that's done, of course, well in advance in their countries. But certainly all the rest.

And, of course, their patient confidentiality will be observed."

"Could you give me an idea of what countries are included?"

"A very, very wide range—from Canada to Saudi Arabia," he smiled almost visualizing the headlines Benjamin would write.

"And even a little Mideast thrown in I assume?" Al smiled back. Sam just shrugged and said "'why not"? Al heard that visitors will also include Sudanese, Palestinians and Pakistanis, and, of course, those from the Bahamas and Colombia.

Al was on his security cell phone immediately upon returning to his hotel room to fill Joe in on this interesting conversation with the PR director.

In noting the time and place of arrival, Benjamin asked a question bothering him for some time. "Joe—why the hell doesn't the INS get involved with this? Like everyone else, these guys must have to check in with U.S. Customs."

"We can't rely on them, unc. Check your newspapers, you'll find there's too many loopholes the terrorists and druggies have been getting through.

If you can help keep track of their activities, including their medical checkups—and bloodwork—it'll sure help all of us."

"Okay, I'll be there whenever possible. You know, though, unlike you and Johnson I don't carry a gun or badge to get around."

"Super. That could also get you into lots of trouble and I don't want my favorite uncle hurt…or worse. Perhaps you could pull your hat down further to hide your bald spot, put your sun glasses on and use that great smile of yours to help open some doors."

The arrival day was sunny enough to justify wearing sun glasses. Benjamin, hidden away in the waiting crowd, nearly had to squint to see the silver jet airliner make a smooth landing at the clinic's international airport. He also had to wiggle his way around some of the observers to get a close look at those getting off the plane.

When he did see them, his jaw dropped. "My god, they look so dignified—there's both men and women aboard—kings and queens," he muttered. Almost every man going down the steps of the plane had shades, beards or mustaches. Most of the women wore burqas or some form of facial scarf. Al tried to remember the main features of Beck described by his nephew: small but very erect, usually with a cigarette dangling from his lips, a caucasian, and sometimes having a slight limp. Not much to go on. But if you're close enough, you can tell it's him by his cold stare that shakes your very soul, his nephew often reminded him.

None of those leaving the plane related much to this description. They were all mostly tall. But only one was smoking, and smaller than the others. And this is the one Benjamin kept an eye on. It wasn't until they all arrived at the airport gate when Al got a better view of this smoker and noticed he also had a little limp.

But how the hell could you look into his eyes? thought Benjamin as he strolled casually along with the rest of the greeters and watched the group boldly shake hands with city and clinic officials eager to be part of the welcoming committee. After this pomp and ceremony they were all whisked away in big black limousines to the waiting clinic.

About the only time this strange mixed group got away from the sight of Al was when they squeezed into an elevator escorted by clinic security personnel. He watched it stop at the fourth floor—where most important visitors sign in.

At this time, all Al could do was to find a remote corner to call Joe from his cell phone and let him know where Beck might be. It was nearly impossible for Kavinsky's aging uncle to race up the many stairs. And waiting for the next elevators could take a very long time, allowing the group to go quickly elsewhere.

Al was reassured by Kavinsky. "That's okay unc. We have that floor covered with a DEA agent. We knew that's where they'd be taken first. Just let me know which one you suspect at this time, at least this gives us a good start."

His uncle nearly clicked off his cell phone upon hearing the doors of the elevator open again when it returned to the main floor. But no one got off or on.

"Hard to tell, Joe. But I think it's the guy with a bit of a limp. He may still be smoking but I doubt if the docs would allow that. He also has big sun glasses and a slightly red beard. I couldn't get close enough to tell if he has those green eyes you were mentioning."

"Okay unc—the agent may be able to close in on him. Call me again in a few minutes and I'll let you know how things up here are progressing. In the meantime, play it safe. Beck probably has a few henchmen with him to spot anyone who may be after him."

"Yeah—and maybe a few hench girls," added Al.

"Whoops—you mean there are women in that group?" responded Joe in surprise.

"Sure are—but mostly covered up in robes."

"I don't think the DEA was expecting that, unc."

"Yeah, nor was the clinic PR guy—nor my pen pal Smiley."

Kavinsky advised his uncle to stay with the group as much as possible without causing any suspicion, and let the DEA guide with them do her thing.

"Her—you mean he's a she?" asked Al almost out loud.

"One of the greeters—the very cute one, the escort in the elevator."

"Yeah—I noticed her—how couldn't you? Good thing the group has a few others like her to carry on some women talk."

"How do I get in touch with this undercover female?"

"You don't. I was told by Johnson that she'll get in touch with you when the time is right. Gotta go now unc…good hunting!"

Al just kind of loafed around the entranceway waiting for the group to return. In the meantime, he had the chance to look at nearly all the plaques, honors, and acclaim also hanging around that area in tribute to the great docs and donors who helped to make the renowned clinic such a noted global medical site.

When the elevator doors finally opened again, Al immediately spotted the cute escort who beckoned her passengers out. All he could think at the time, however, was "wow—what a babe."

CHAPTER 16

While this was going on, Joe was receiving a report from the Bloomington police department on the license identification of the woman suspect fleeing from the mall. It was somewhat difficult, since the car she was driving was a rental and the name she used was not the same as that on her driver's license.

The name on the license was Salid Ashid while the rental car company had her listed as Sally Ashton. Neither name could be found in the Twin Cities' phone books, Moreover. Joe also checked with the state transportation department that also had no record of either name in their large files of authorized Minnesota drivers.

"How did she get by without one?" Kavinsky muttered to himself. One way, he figured, was to produce her own driver's license. But the traffic cop who stopped her said it looked very authentic. Another way, was to assume that she's the girl friend of Amad and only he would know her real whereabouts to contact her. For that matter, she most likely was a member of the same cell group that Amad belongs to, he reasoned.

But how do you arrest Amad without letting the entire cell know?

Kavinsky was scratching his head over this question when his annoying counterpart, Dave Paulson, knocked on his office cubicle.

Paulson, almost whispering and looking around as though someone may be eaves-dropping, asked Kavinsky what he thought of the precinct's rookie detective. It was as though he was tuned in to Joe's mind. "He's a strange cat isn't he Joe, stays around the office nearly until it closes and then goes out to prowl."

Joe acted as though he was surprised but interested in what Paulson may be saying next. "From what I know, he's a single guy and quite a swinger. Can you imagine him in a singles bar—he may have a harem for that matter," Paulson chuckled.

"Does he even have a girl friend?" asked Joe taking advantage of Paulson's comments to know more about Amad.

"Yeah—I saw him several times with the same one. She's mostly in Muslim wraps. "A burqa," Joe corrected. "Whatever," shrugged Paulson. "I asked Amad who she is, but all he said was that he met her at a dance—hell can you imagine dancing in that long gown she wears?"

Joe smiled just to keep Dave talking on this subject. "So you never ever caught her name?"

"Matter of fact, I did Joe—just a few minutes ago, right here in our department. It was quite by accident. I bumped into them going around the corner while studying a report on one of our downtown hustlers.

The name is Sally, mind you. It's gotta be a fake. She's as Mideast as they come."

"Did you catch her last name," asked an impatient Joe.

"All I recall is that it sounded somewhat like Ash. I checked this out on Amad's note pad when he left—but could hardly read his writing. They outta make these foreigners learn English."

"Suppose she lives close near Amad?" asked Joe to keep Dave trying to describe this suspect.

"No, matter of fact her address was also scratched on his note pad. She's way out in Woodbury, that western suburb."

To end this confidential chat with Paulson, Joe played on his ego by flattering him for being such a slueth. "No wonder you're such a great detective Dave—you really know how to size 'em up. About the only thing you didn't get is her address." He laughed and walked away, leaving the arrogant Paulson upset.

"What do you mean...here it is: 2064 Windsor. You don't get by old Dave so easy."

Joe knew his strategy was working. "And I guess you never want to leave any notes around where old Dave can see them," he remarked rising from his chair and leading Paulson out of his cubicle.

CHAPTER 17

Kavinsky felt it was time to get the DEA more involved. Johnson, however, was still against making any arrests in case this might jeopardize the progress already underway at the clinic. However, he believed they may have their man already when the person with the same DNA as Beck's went into the lab for blood work.

But much to the surprise of all authorities focusing on the little man smoking and limping, there was no DNA match with Beck's at all—nor was there with any of the group. It was as if all the preparatory work to making an arrest was wasted. At this point they couldn't help feel a little guilty for My Guy's death.

To soften the blow of perhaps screwing up, and greatly disappointed about coming up with still no trace of their suspect, Joe, Terry and Hermes commiserated at a pub miles away from the precinct station. There wasn't much explanation, since all were still confused over how this could happen—considering everyone in that arrival group who checked in showed no trace of blood like Beck's.

"I can't understand it. Absolutely every person up there had to have routine in-patient blood work before they could undergo any treatment," emphasized Joe. Terry added, "except for the escorts and including our agent...who personally saw this being done. Hell, the only ones not having their fingers pricked were their wives or other women they flew in with who needed to be with them."

Johnson's comment stopped Kavinsky as he was about to order another round. "By the way, did we have identification on each of those ladies? Most were in shrouds, you know."

"Specific arrangements were made for them at the order of the INS—they were to be treated as visiting dignitaries. As far as I know they were also to be given the same VIP treatment as their husbands—or girl friends," noted Johnson.

"You don't suppose...?" Joe couldn't finish his thought when Johnson interrupted with—"that one of them might be Beck in a dress?"

"He'd do anything to weasel his way into the states. For all we know those others could be his terrorists," Hermes said, as though reading Joe's mind. "We outta check that out when we can. I can alert the local clinic police chief."

"Whoa gentlemen!" cautioned Johnson. "Keep in mind they're here as guests of our nation. And as such they are under special federal protection—much like diplomatic immunity."

"Well, do you have any better idea?" Hermes asked looking sternly at the DEA agent. "We can't just let those guys run amok. Hell, they're already around here and into our own great Mall . I'm also dedicated to protecting our people."

Listening to all this, Kavinsky quickly jumped into the conversation with an opinion that bordered on some wild imagination.

"Hey guys, remember the old saying: 'It Takes a Thief to Catch a Thief'?. Maybe we should try using Amad's girl friend to help capture him. After all, she probably knows all about whose behind those dresses.

"It certainly isn't up to us to undress them...but Sally, or whoever she is, can see who it might be while she's in the lady's lounge or rest room with them."

"How can we get her to do that, Joe? She'll be on to us and give us all away," Hermes shrugged.

"Tact, gentlemen…very good tact," Johnson advised, breaking into the conversation.

"Like what?" asked Joe. "Like tricking Sally into thinking Beck wants to see her," suggested Johnson.

"How the hell are you going to do that?" inquired Kavinsky.

"I'm not sure yet—perhaps the CIA, FBI or Homeland Security can help me figure it out. But off hand I'd say we should work through Amad. Maybe offer him a big reward for betraying his comrades and less time in prison."

"He wouldn't do that. He likes being a detective," the police chief noted. "It also gets him closer to what the cops are secretly planning against the druggies and terrorists."

"If he thought this would mean a promotion and a chance to get out of that terrorist cell he's in, do you think this might influence him?" questioned Terry.

"It may be worth the try," Joe said. "What's he got to lose?—we have the goods on him that he may have tried to poison me. If we let that charge drop it may be an incentive to go along with us. You never know, he may have just tasted the coffee, and the guy next to him could have been the one that dropped in the poison."

"And if he doesn't cooperate?" asked Kavinsky.

"We'll lock him up," said the chief.

"But that would let Sally, or Salid—or whoever—to know we're on to her and the whole Beck scenario," Joe pointed out.

"So what?" Johnson commented—surprising Kavinsky. We're at a point now that someone should blow the whistle—every minute that group is here the entire country may be in danger. It's anyone's guess now what they're up to."

CHAPTER 18

Trying to accomplish this plan, however, was tougher than first thought. Since Amad considered himself somewhat of a pal of Paulson's at work, it was Dave's job to bring him to the chief's office where Terry and Joe were waiting for him.

Paulson, little known for his tact, was somehow able to convince Amad that the chief wanted to see them both regarding a special assignment. On this pretense, they met Johnson while the chief stood by to let them know he was supporting what was about to be discussed.

As soon as Terry was introduced as being with the DEA, Amad's dark face paled and frowned as he reached for the top of his chair for support. The chief asked him to sit down and then both he and Johnson began their attempt at persuasion. All Amad did at first was to hear the case against him and the way he might lessen some of the serious consequences.

At first, Amad opposed giving any suggested help to the plan discussed. However, when the offers to attempt to lighten the penalties were made he quit shaking his head no and began to listen intently, as though realizing they had him where they wanted and he was better off cooperating.

But would Salid go along with this? Amad wasn't sure. However, he agreed to talk with her after Terry and the chief assured him that she also would be given leniency for help in bringing Beck to justice, before he could do any more harm to the country and perhaps even the world.

By the time this confidential meeting was over, detailed strategy was made to assure the safety of Amad and his girl friend, if she agrees with their plan, as well as the close communications that would be essential between them and the feds and local authorities to carry out this operation successfully. If this fails, because of Amad or Salid, they would be prosecuted to the fullest extent—perhaps life in prison or even death for attempted murder and acts of terrorism.

The next step would be to monitor their progress to find Beck—even if he's disguised like a woman—so he can be revealed in time to avoid his terrorism.

To make sure Amad followed through with this, Paulson was assigned to accompany him to the clinic and stay with him as though the two were on official police duty. The trip, in an unmarked squad car, was to start that very afternoon. This allowed only several hours for Amad to convince Salid to cooperate.

As Paulson waited outside in the car, Amad rang the doorbell at Salid's apartment. Using small but powerful binoculars, Paulson saw her appearing in a sheer, nearly transparent nightie greeting her boy friend. He couldn't help but think she was a far cry from the cloaked conservative Kavinsky described to him.

It seemed a long time before this strange couple left the house, keeping Paulson wondering what indeed was happening. He fingered his gun wondering how friendly they would be after their private conference. He knew Amad wasn't armed since his gun was taken at the precinct, but he wasn't sure if the girl might be.

However, surprisingly both were smiling as they approached the car. The moment the girl reached the car door Paulson searched her for weapons but was assured by Amad that both were harmless. They then got into the squad car and, with Amad driving, headed to the clinic while Paulson kept his gun handy.

As all this was happening, Paulson also had his two-way police radio turned on. Like a taxi cab driver, he alerted precinct headquarters of the time of their departure and expected arrival. This gave him another feeling of security since he could immediately notify headquarters if any problems occur, including any acts of violence this unpredictable couple may want to cause.

Also helping to provide Paulson with an extra sense of security was his knowing that Kavinsky was following in an unmarked car.

When they drove up to the clinic both vehicles parked almost next to one another, in an alley used mostly for medical delivery trucks. Joe let Paulson enter first with his passengers. He then put on horned-rim glasses and a small mustache that tickled his nose. He felt like Groucho Marx as he walked to meet his uncle.

Joe startled Benjamin, proudly wearing a special press badge from the clinic PR director, when he tapped his uncle's shoulder. Al was checking out Paulson's "guests" from behind one of the clinic's elegant hallway pillars. But he quickly recognized his nephew when he whispered jokingly,"stick 'em up."

"Good lord Joey, you're going to give me a heart attack yet."

"Just wanted to see how alert you are unc," chuckled Joe.

"I see you brought your buddies with you. Good, they'll find the group of dignitaries—and hopefully our hidden suspect—on the top floor at the in-patient area," reported Al.

"Paulson's going to check out soon," noted Joe. W'ell then leave it up to the DEA." Just as he said this, the elevator doors opened again and the pretty undercover escort beckoned Amad and his friend in for a ride to the top.

Before the doors closed, however, Joe also hopped into the elevator, surprising the escort. "You got a gun or something?" he whispered.

"I never travel alone," she replied, lifting her skirt a little to disclose a revolver as well as a knife and very attractive legs. He patted his gun to show her she also had backup help if needed.

"Who's your boss," he asked to further confirm her credentials.

"Terry Johnson—and yours is chief Hermes."

Enough said—from then until stopping at the crowded check-in floor, the elevator seemed filled with quiet and a sense of security considering the sinister ones accompanying them. Joe was more relaxed, knowing his friend Johnson was involved in making all the necessary precautionary arrangements.

Kavinsky stayed in the back of the elevator as the others got off, hoping not to be recognized by any of those in the waiting room who he may have met during his undercover work in the Bahamas. He immediately pushed the down button and headed back to the first floor to meet his uncle.

The elevator stopped only once enroute, to let a dark-skinned lady on who was dressed in casual western clothes. He smiled, but she frowned. He wanted to hurry up the elevator. When he got to the main floor, however, Al had disappeared.

Funny, thought Joe, his uncle had orders to remain exactly at the spot he was to meet him. It must have been very important why he would ever leave his assigned "station" Joe figured, recalling his uncle's stories of always being an obedient soldier—even if it meant charging up a hill dodging bullets. Above all, he would never leave his guard post.

Kavinsky quickly alerted Johnson on his cell phone of his missing uncle. Terry made note of this and tried assuring Joe that Al will probably return shortly, although both were also thinking of what could happen if Beck's gang made off with him. Joe recalled that Al mentioned he was talking with the clinic PR director about this event and wondered if he met with his uncle again for some reason.

A quick call to the clinic's public relations department connected him with Sam Stone, who could only confirm that Al had a press pass to roam around the complex but he had no idea as to where Benjamin might be at this time.

"If you see him Mr. Kavinsky please let him know we'd also like him to attend our welcoming presentation for the dignitaries at 10 a.m. in our international room. We plan to give them an official toast with the best of our imported champagne, or non-alcoholic beverage—or whatever they prefer, of course. I'm sure Al would agree it would be a great picture for his proposed article and, of course, an excellent publicity photo opt for the clinic," he grinned. When Joe gave Terry this status report, Johnson's creative mind took over. Why not get a saliva sample off the glasses used for the toast from each person in the group—including their lady friends? The DEA could then try for a match with Beck's sample that was obtained by the late My Guy.

He tried contacting Paulson to arrange for Amad or for his "Gal Sal"—which was the label the DEA pinned on her—to attend this celebrity welcome toast. Amad, determined to carry out all orders to obtain some leniency from the feds, informed Paulson that she was in the nearby ladies rest room with most of the other women guests already primping for this event.

"Sal" had never met Beck so she only had the sketchy information Terry and Joe gave her about his appearance. But she did tell Paulson that one of the so-called spouses went immediately into a stall and remained there until the others were ready to leave the restroom.

This was the same person who had a very slight limp, she noted, and the only one who spoke with a cigarette hanging from "her" lips.

The big tip-off, however, were the hairy legs…revealed when the suspect pulled up sliding panty hose that began falling down to large pointed shoes. Amad's girl friend turned her gaze away from the mirror the suspect was looking at before those cold green eyes could get a fix on her.

"I think we've got him—or her—chief," reported Paulson on his cell phone to Terry after being updated by the girl informer regarding the strange man masquerading as a woman. "Watch for the suspect leaving the women's restroom. He'll be followed by Salid. This has to be Beck."

"Good, but don't try an arrest yet, cautioned Johnson who couldn't help but think Joe's uncle Al may be missing, and perhaps even being held as a hostage for terrorist negotiations.

"Just keep a close eye on your suspect, but make sure he gets to the welcome party and has a drink. We want to run a DNA on his saliva." Paulson frowned hearing this and muttered to himself, "God what a yukky thing to have to do."

CHAPTER 19

✾

Joe continued to be concerned over his uncle's whereabouts, especially when he didn't show up for toasting the so-called prestigious visitors. He could imagine Al all tied up by now waiting for his captors to make a call to the feds requesting them to back off from pursuing their leader—or else.

He quietly put out a 1040 APB search report via his cell phone and was assured by his precinct that it would be handled as discreetly as possible, making certain the visiting clinic bunch wouldn't hear about it. Local police were notified and even sent special undercover and other non-uniform personnel to check this out.

But God, what was Joe going to tell aunt Kay? He decided it best to delay contacting her until reports came in from the searching parties.

One party not participating in this, of course, was being held in tribute to the visitors on the top floor. As glasses were held high in the toast to their first trip to the clinic, Amad's girl friend let Terry know who she thought was Beck—the shy little thing standing in a corner shrouded in a robe, like most all the other spouses afraid to sip anything that might offend their husbands.

As this was happening, corks were popping as the undercover DEA lady made it a point to fill the goblets of each of the other cloaked women remaining in the background. They almost smiled in unison as though rehearsed to do so as exotic refreshments were also offered.

The clinic president, standing next to his smiling PR man, saluted the guests with words of warm welcome as their glasses were refilled and more tasty snacks served. Joe couldn't help but think how happy his uncle would have been to be munching on these goodies.

However, although Kavinsky along with others had grim thoughts of what Al may be going through, his uncle was actually nowhere near danger. In fact, he was also nibbling on a snack—in a phone booth. Seems Kavinsky's wife received a message from the U.S. Postal Service that prompted Sarah to try to reach Joe without success. She finally decided the next step to contact him would be through his uncle who she knew would be somewhere nearby. Fortunately, she recalled that Benjamin had been working with the clinic's PR department and with its help was able to locate Al.

The hotel bellman over-reacted by telling Benjamin he had an emergency phone call. This was the only reason Al left his post. He forgot and left his cell phone in his car and was upset by having to rush to a phone booth in another area. He calmed down, however, when Sarah said she just wanted to have him inform his nephew that the Post Office wanted her and Joe to meet with its postal inspectors at their Twin Cities headquarters on a very important matter that couldn't be discussed over the phone.

Intent on getting this information to his nephew, Benjamin rushed to get his cell phone and made a call to Joe from his car. Kavinsky, however, seemed more annoyed over the ringing of his phone than the news. Although a long way from where the action was, he wanted to avoid as much attention as possible.

But when Joe heard Al's voice he sighed in relief. "My God unc where have you been? You've got everyone searching for you. We thought by now you might be crucified upside upside down by that mysterious gang of visitors."

"Slow down, Joey. I'm okay, but I had to take a phone call from your bride. She said it's important to get in touch with the postal inspector's office. They want to discuss something with you."

"The postal inspectors—what the hell are they up to? We certainly don't need another group of feds involved in this. Call them back, unc, and make any excuse you can to get them off our backs. We sure don't want them.We've got enough feds bumping into one another here already."

Before clicking off, Al asked Joe if it would be okay for him to come up and see what's going on at the gala visitor reception, since he was getting bored and tired just hanging around near the elevator. He almost dropped the phone, however, when his nephew nearly yelled in a scolding manner "No—damnit. You stay hidden. It would be best if you pretended to still be among the missing."

"If word gets around that the police think Beck's group has you in their clutches, that gang may want to use you as a pawn even though they haven't got the slightest idea right now where the hell you are. They may come looking for you, and we're not about to give them any opportunities."

"But Joey—that's an awful long-shot. How do you know they even know I'm around the clinic?" Al asked. "Word's already gotten out to the authorities and ten to one it's spread around.to them by now," explained Joe. He insisted, "Let me handle this, unc. I'll inform aunt Kay of what we're up to. At least she'll know you're okay. Just stay out of sight—or get the hell home and hide."

"What about the Post Office?"

"Have Sarah call them back—or better yet have her hear them out even if means taking the trouble to drive to their damn office. I'm sure it's just a simple matter—perhaps we forgot to put enough stamps on our last letter," chuckled Joe before clicking off.

Al was still holding the phone to his ear after Joe left, thinking his nephew was awfully casual about all of this. He didn't quite follow the logic about hiding out. About all he could figure out from this strategy was that perhaps some of Beck's group would be more inclined to blab to let authorities know they had nothing to do with Al's disappearance. Maybe that's what his nephew was trying to say—whatever it was, he was sure the DEA was also aware of it.

CHAPTER 20

While all this excitement was going on, Jerry Donovan, an inspector of the U.S. 5th Postal District, was sitting back in his office chair almost twiddling his thumbs waiting for a call back from Sarah. At least, he felt, this was a nice break from the exceptionally busy times the Post Office was currently involved with relating to the anthrax scare and such annoying problems as the public's reaction to a recent hike in the cost of stamps.

Donovan was nearing retirement and figured he didn't need any more pressures. But he always felt he was in the right job. Ever since he was a kid he was always interested in stamps. His dad took him to stamp collector stores and helped him with albums that still remain in his bookshelves at home. Some he was especially proud of—indeed he was sure his collection could bring a nice price. But Jerry wasn't about to sell any and encouraged his son to carry on his beloved stamp collecting after he's gone.

As usual, Donovan was one of the first to be called in to any major investigation involving the mail. His track record in helping to solve postal crimes was as outstanding as his finding of rare stamps. He was also noted for finding the reasons—and the persons involved—for misuse of the mail relating to everything from sending indecent or dangerous materials to downright mail fraud schemes affecting numerous individuals and businesses throughout the metro and suburban areas of the Twin Cities.

This is why he was assigned to investigate the causes and consequences of the recent fire that nearly destroyed the mail truck that was on its way around the neighborhood where Joe and Sarah had just rented a home.

Donovan kept looking at some of the items damaged from smoke and fire, wondering why this erupted in the middle of winter and even after the truck, like the rest of that postal station's fleet, was given a recent overhaul. He knew the driver had a good track record, and was commended for his attempts at putting out the blaze that apparently began from an overheated engine despite wintry weather.

Most of the mail was still smoldering from the extreme heat. Donovan laid some out on top of his big desk and almost had to cover his nose with his handkerchief to avoid coughing from the smoke as he tried to examine items more closely. As he did so, his keen collector's eyes couldn't help but be attracted by a still colorful stamp that stood out among all the others. It was from Bermuda.

Because of the poor condition of the envelope Donovan could barely make out the address, which was somewhat scrawled to begin with. But with the help of a high-powered magnifying glass he was able to put together the name. He very carefully opened the fragile fire-marred envelope and looked inside…what he saw prompted him to make his first unsuccessful call to the Kavinsky residence.

Looking at his watch again, realizing it may take a long time to hear back from either Sarah or Joe, he felt the urge for what he called a "stamp hunt." He hooked on his cell phone and went to one of his favorite stamp collector stores at the nearby mall. He often liked to browse there and then get a skim latte coffee as a treat. But he couldn't keep his mind from drifting to what he had seen inside Sarah's envelope.

In the meantime, Al Benjamin found a safer place to hide.

He went deep into the bowels of the medical clinic, near the MRI tube, and sat there wondering what his next sneaky move should be to keep out of sight. He stifled a yawn while reading an early morning newspaper he got on the way into the clinic. As usual, there were reports on terrorism running rampant and warnings about where the next attacks will be, and even about expected suicide bombers.

Al just shook his head as he continued perusing the paper, thinking "where and when the hell is it all going to end?" At least he figured he was safe. The structure around his area was probably made with titanium steel and anti-radioactive materials that no man could ever penetrate.

But this reminded him that Beck was reportedly dressed like a woman, and if anyone could slither into a security area it could be that weasel. He almost shuddered thinking of this possibility. If that wasn't enough to upset him, he also began recalling the anthrax mail scare attributed to the terrorists.

Moreover, thinking about the mail brought him back to wondering what the hell the postal inspector wanted to talk to Joe about. He recalled that the caller sounded very serious, almost excited about what he wanted to discuss with his nephew and wife.

Al chuckled quietly over his nephew's first reaction to this. In no way did he want another federal agent to bump into on this case, especially the Post Office which so many jump on when there's even a late mail delivery. Hell, thought Al, there's already probably the FBI, CIA, INS, BATF, HOME SECURITY and ATF, besides the DEA up there with Joe, not to mention the local office of protocol for international visitors. His thoughts were suddenly interrupted, however, by the sound of a door being opened in the chamber adjoining the MRI. Al made sure to remain in his dark corner as the door creaked open more. He wasn't sure who or what was there until conversation began. About all he could make out were three persons, each with gowns. One seemed to be a doctor, the other probably a lab worker, and the other a nurse.

At first, he couldn't understand what was being said. The chatter almost seemed to be in pig latin. Realizing the clinic attracts numerous foreign doctors, medical students, registered nurses and technicians, he figured they were just discussing some of the many health problems being dealt with. But why in this dark chamber?

However, he finally heard something in English that was very familiar. It sounded like the name Beck A few moments later someone said "yes, and they're upstairs." Benjamin tried to tip-toe very quietly to a spot where he could get a closer look at those doing the talking. Not wanting to blow his cover, while peering around a wall separating him from the mysterious talkers he found a hole near one of the support beams enabling him to get a bird's eye view of what was going on. Although he could barely see this mysterious trio, he noted they were all still in official blue scrub uniforms as though just out of surgery. The one doing most of the talking apparently was the doctor, he looked very important with a stethoscope around his neck. Those doing most of the listening included a woman whom he thought he knew. She still had surgical goggles and an operating room mask dangling under her chin.

CHAPTER 21

The other guy could have been from anywhere in the clinic. It seemed, however, that he might be from one of the labs since Benjamin noticed he was holding a glass lab slide, of the type used under medical microscopes. Al's interest really piqued, however, when he heard the words "blood sample" mentioned by the lab guy.

Benjamin's mind began to run wild. Could it be that this professional-looking trio was controlling the blood work being done to find Beck? Were they planning something, or was it already done? And why were they down in this dark remote "hole" instead of upstairs mingling with their peers?

As Benjamin was keeping a keen eye on this bunch, his nephew was observing the group of esteemed visitors on the top floor, ready to go their separate ways to be examined for the special health problems—that supposedly brought them to the clinic in the first place.

And as Al kept his distance from the group to avoid recognition, he also hoped he was emphatic enough with his uncle to stay out of sight—or go back home—before anyone could figure he also was spying on them. As he stuffed the phone number of the postal inspector in his pocket, thinking this could wait, he noticed the VIP visitors starting to leave the reception.

Upstairs, Kavinsky was confused over what person to follow. When the guy with the limp returned to the rest room, Joe chuckled over the thought that he may be adding lipstick.

Growing impatient, Joe looked for a more comfortable place to sit, not knowing for sure when or how long of a wait he'd have before this guy—or gal—would leave the restroom. He found a newspaper and noticed his uncle had his byline on a story about police and racial profiling. Fortunately, his photo wasn't included. That would almost be the last straw, Joe thought, in letting this group identify Al and then god knows what would happen if they spotted his uncle.

After perusing the entire paper, even the society section which Joe seldom reads, he reached for a magazine on what's happening in the clinic's community. But by the time he finished scanning every article and advertisement promoting the variety of things to buy and do in between health checkups, he was almost ready to go into the restroom and see what the hell "he or she" was doing to take so long.

When the door to the restroom finally opened, out came an elderly lady. Joe was disappointed, hoping it would be his man—no longer in a dress. He strolled in back of her and then boldly asked if there was anyone else in the room. Startled by this brash young man, whose fake mustache was now a bit cockeyed, she at first hesitated as though this was none of his business, but then emphatically said no. When asked if there was another door out of the restroom, she said yes—that it led to the back exit, near the steps down to the second floor.

"Damn!" Joe almost said out loud, startling the old lady. He realized that bastard Beck escaped and was now probably already on the street starting to terrorize America with his drugs.

Joe's first inclination was to alert Al to be on the lookout at the exits since his last encounter with his uncle was around that area. But he remembered that his uncle was ordered to stay hidden and he sure didn't want to blow his cover.

He next thought was to contact Johnson, who perhaps could quickly call his fellow DEA agents to catch Beck on the run. But how could he describe him? Was he still disguised as a limping little lady, or was he once again the real he-man, with a scowl on his face, ice-cold eyes and, as always, with a cigarette? For that matter, he could probably avoid limping by wearing a special set of shoes.

But where the hell would he be going? And what's the fastest way to get the word out to protect those in the way? Such questions poured into the head of Kavinsky as he tried to determine the best strategy to be one-step ahead of this evil-doer.

Out of sheer frustration, he turned to his cell phone for some answers. It was as though his fingers automatically did the work. They clicked onto Al's phone numbers even though Kavinsky was in favor of keeping his uncle out of all this.

The dial tone lasted only a second or so before Al's voice was heard. In almost a whisper, Benjamin said simply: "Yeah Joe—can't talk much. Be brief and very quiet." Kavinsky wondered why his uncle was whispering as he quickly gave the alarm that Beck was on the loose.

In fact, Joe somewhat feared for his uncle's sanity when Al calmly responded: "Don't worry Joey, I know where's he's headed—and why."

At about the same time Al was briefing his nephew about what he knew, based on what he overheard as the medical trio gossiped near the area where he was hiding, several muscular guys were leading Beck from the clinic into a waiting limousine.

They were on their way north on U.S. 52 N even before Al could inform his nephew that their destination was the Twin Cities. He overheard the trio in the remote chambers mention Beck was to meet with leading drug kingpins, and then if possible they would leave the mall in ruins as a protest to freedom and U.S. liberalism.

About all Joe could do while Al was talking was nod his head, as though agreeing with every word being said and that someone else was with him taking notes. His uncle wasn't going crazy, he realized. It all came together now. As the DEA warned, the Beck gang was aiming at the mall all along but didn't want Joe to get in the way—so they planted the poison in his drink.

Moreover, Al found out the reason there was no DNA evidence from the blood work The sinister medical personnel who he heard discussing this probably destroyed all the paperwork evidence.

"Too bad you didn't get this on tape, unc."

"Ah—but I did Joe. A good reporter never leaves home without taking his little portable recorder."

Recorder or not, Joe was stymied in his attempt to track down the group whisking Beck away. He reported this to Terry who also was baffled over how to catch up with their get-away car. After thinking this over, however, Joe snapped his fingers and asked if the vehicle was parked in one of the clinic's many ramps.

"No—we checked that out, too. Plus, we found that the attendants are just there to stamp the parking cards and take money. No questions asked."

"How about the official VIP ramp?"

"You mean they have one?"

"I'll bet they do, and that the attendant may have to note names of the VIPs arriving and even get their license numbers and times they depart."

"Damn—if you're right Joe we have something to go on at least, and hopefully cut them off on the way to the cities."

Although Kavinsky was rather annoyed by having to tell these sharp DEA guys how to do their job, he realized he was used to visiting the clinic from time to time when visiting sick relatives and became familiar with some of that institution's parking regulations. It was now up to Terry to figure a way to get the name of the driver and to intercept the car with the help of police around the area where they may be seen.

Terry was one jump ahead of Joe. His agent, disguised as a parking attendant, almost immediately got back to him with the license number information, since he personally recorded each VIP car when entering and leaving the ramp. He said "It was a dark blue Chrysler van, probably a Voyager about 2001, with tinted windows."

"Yeah—but what about the driver's name and the people he had in it?" inquired Johnson.

"We got the driver's name, but there were too many others to get."

After giving Johnson the information he obtained, the agent then added, "by the way who's the gal that's with those tough-looking dudes?"

"Gal—you mean they weren't all males?"

"Nope—she was all woman and a real winner, too," added the observant young agent.

"Ever see her before?"

"I'm not sure. In some ways I thought I recognized her."

But after a little more thinking he asked, "wasn't she with that spouse group at the clinic and earlier with that Amad fella from the precinct?"

Johnson hesitated, causing the agent to ask if he was still on the phone. "Yeah," replied Terry. "I may know this girl, too. And she may be our ace in the hole."

Tragedy interfered, however, only about an hour after this phone call took place. It was announced by the highway patrol which had some very bad news.

"Officer down! officer down!" was all the excited voice on the other end was yelling from patrol headquarters.

"DEA responding, DEA responding," was Johnson's answer.

Having heard the "Officer Down" warning before, Terry knew that calm and slow communications were necessary in such cases.

"Patrolman shot and killed four miles from Cannon River on Highway 52N. Fired upon by driver when stopped for speeding. Be on alert for dark blue van filled with passengers. Believe headed north to Twin Cities."

Johnson kept holding the phone hoping that the dispatcher reporting this would eventually talk to him directly following this general alert. After issuing the report at least several times, the voice on the other end gave his name and offered to explain more to Terry.

"Are they now being pursued by police, what's the license number and was there a female in the vehicle?" These were questions Terry quickly asked knowing that whoever was on the other end was very busy and emotional.

"They're being chased by patrol cars now, from both directions, but are many miles from them sir. No license number yet. Already went through Cannon River, nearly hit kid on bike. Patrol helicopter asked to help spot them," the dispatcher reported.

"It must be Sal—she's pulled a fast one on us," declared Johnson.

"The only female around who could get that close to Beck would be the Muslim girl who the DEA trusted to spy for us," Terry reasoned. He recalled that Salid Ashid promised to help bring Beck to justice if she would be granted leniency for her role involving the attempted poisoning of Joe to avoid his interfering with Beck's Midwest mission.

Kavinsky was as surprised as Terry when he received an update on this. But he couldn't help but wonder why the woman passenger would want to dig even a deeper hole for herself by being an accomplice in this matter. On the other hand, he thought, she may be actually riding along as their hostage.

It took longer than expected to get any helpful information from the agent at the clinic site where the car was parked. Unfortunately, the in-and-out records for that day were among those placed in the wrong file. The attendant was quite certain, however, that they could find them soon. In the meantime, all that Johnson and Kavinsky could do was hope the authorities could stop the suspects at some of the little towns along the way. "But cripes," said Joe, "We're not sure if it's really the car we want. The cops didn't catch the license number—it could be just a hit-and-run case—just another group of bandits rather than Beck and his gang."

Kavinsky was glad to let Al know via cell phone that he could come out from hiding now. Both realized it was extremely lucky that Al had overheard what was being planned by the three medical personnel discussing this near his hiding place.

But Joe still had to confer with Johnson regarding how to deal with this. Who are they? what are they up to? and are they really part of the clinic's medical staff?

Both agreed that it would be best, if not most diplomatic and politically correct, to let Al inquire about this with his friend the clinic PR director. After checking in with his wife to let her know everything's okay, Al contacted Stone and, under pretense of discussing some of the information he obtained from the VIP visit for his intended feature on the clinic, he was invited to sit down with Stone for lunch that very noon.

Benjamin was impressed with the elegant surroundings of the lunch room, considered the famous clinic's executive dining room on the top floor of the clinic. He was rather disappointed, however, that Stone brought a guest.

"Al, I'd like you to meet our VP of international relations, Dr. Iverson. Since we're talking about your upcoming feature article I thought he could add some of his thoughts to it all. Dr. Iverson has been with us for many years and has been involved with our great success."

CHAPTER 22

For more than an hour, Benjamin had to think up questions for answers he knew would never be printed even if he was serious about writing a feature.

He could only hope Iverson had some other appointments soon and that the entire afternoon wouldn't be tied up with this pretended interview.

The subject of DNA was brought up, along with how important information can be derived from blood and saliva samples. In fact, noted Iverson proudly, some physicians envision a day when a patient's DNA can be stored on a credit-card-sized chip to help prescribe therapy.

Following several more cups of coffee, with the doctor doing the pouring—which surprised Al since too much was usually considered bad for the health—Iverson got up and excused himself to meet with some global gurus regarding foreign medical affairs. Al was hoping this wouldn't break up his meeting with Stone since he didn't have a chance to quiz him yet about the guys he overheard talking downstairs.

Luckily Stone wasn't invited to follow the executive and filled his coffee cup again. Al put up his hand indicating he had enough, but leaned forward with pen and paper to let Stone know he needed more information. "I really want to do a big piece on the clinic Sam, but I'd like to accent it with some more human interest items."

"Like what Al?" asked the PR man with a smile, knowing this would mean an even bigger story for his employer to admire.

"Well for one thing, how much casual time do you allow the docs and lab workers? They must be almost overworked when such a VIP crowd comes here needing immediate attention."

"It's a pleasure for all our staff to be able to host these important people Al. We don't mind at all to work longer and put in as much time and effort to help them—which is why they came here in the first place. Why do you ask?"

Al shrugged his shoulders and replied, "It's nice to know how well you treat both patients and staff Sam and I'd like to make note of that. You know, pointing out that the clinic's got a heart for everyone. I sort of picked up on that when I accidentally heard several of your staff taking time out in the downstairs MRI chambers. They were discussing the blood work being done many floors up."

"Well they don't have to be that vocal about it. After all, this is somewhat of a private and personal visit," said Stone in a rather scolding manner.

"You certainly wouldn't think so the way they were talking so loudly," Al interjected. "I took some notes—they were very interesting and would help the reader know you have some brilliant people working on such special guests."

"We have them working on everyone Al. That's what we're all about. Both kings and ditch diggers—we treat them very well."

"That's great Sam. But I wonder if you could give me the names of those who were doing the talking. I sure would like to give them the credit they deserve."

"What time and where was this happening?" inquired the accommodating Stone.

"About a couple of feet away from the doorway to the MRI room on the bottom floor—near the tube like entrance to the clinic."

"Did one have a doctor's smock on, wear glasses and have a slight scar on his face?"

"Yeah—and the others were in blue scrubs. One held a blood slide and the other a magnifying glass."

"I'm just guessing Al, but I believe that would be Drs. Namid and Hassmo and their nurse Lorena—they were the principals among the blood workers," explained Stone.

"They're very astute—among our best DNA experts," he added.

"Do they always confer so far from their lab?"

"Could be they had a special project down there."

Al then asked for the spelling of their names and as he scribbled this down on his notepad, Stone requested the chance to look over his story copy before going to press.

Keeping in mind that he probably wasn't really going to prepare an article, he circumvented the issue by reminding Stone that newspapers seldom feed copy back to their source for approval prior to printing. However, he further fibbed somewhat by saying he'd try to make it a point to make this an exception since Sam was so obliging.

Almost immediately after lunch, Al called his nephew letting him know the names of the trio he overheard who seemed to be among conspirators in this scenario, and then asked if any headway was made in catching up to the get-away car.

Kavinsky figured the "evil one" was probably entering the outskirts of the Twin Cities by the time he got Al's call. He also realized that there was a good chance that following the shooting they stopped to replace their license plates. The question was where. If it was at a gas station along the way between Cannon River and the ramp to St. Paul there may be some slight hope that a station attendant would still remember the replaced license numbers.

But he also knew this was like drawing straws. It was such slim hope that Joe shrugged it off and asked for a 1040 APB alert to be sent to all highway patrol and suburban and metro police to be on the lookout for the dark blue van with tinted windows, the only thing he had to go on. He urged that no press should be notified.

In re-grouping with his pal Johnson, Joe was also advised that the some of the National Guard was alerted to help capture Beck. Terry was surprised to know from Joe that even the postal service probably wants to be involved. Johnson, like Joe, joked that those being hunted may still be using old 34-cent stamps.

The DEA assigned a special task force to help determine where, and if, the Beck car stopped enroute. They began by mapping out where stations, restaurants, bars, or any other possible stopping-off places might be between the cop shooting and the St. Paul outskirts.

And the major question, of course, was once this bunch got to its destination what would happen? Johnson theorized that they would meet with a variety of co-conspirators dealing with drugs and money laundering, from those in corporate and financial executive positions to those posing as ordinary citizens but running drug operations behind the scenes.

After all, he reminded Joe, money laundering is the process of disguising illegally obtained money so that the funds appear to come from legitimate sources or activities. It occurs in connection with a wide variety of crimes, including not only drug trafficking, but illegal arms sales, robbery, fraud, racketeering and, of course, terrorism.

He warned that a recent estimate by the U.S. State Department puts the amount of worldwide money laundering activity at $1 trillion a year. Beck and his gang must be stopped, since they could further taint the nation's financial markets by using the U.S. financial system to facilitate terrorism or other crimes.

"Wow," was all Joe could muster up after hearing Terry's comments. "We've gotta halt them in their tracks. In fact, beat them to their first meeting place."

"Exactly Joe. That's why we're trying to tail them so closely. Wherever they stop to do their so-called business is where we have to cut them off before they can do it."

When Joe relayed this to his uncle, Benjamin reminded Joe that he had given the names of the mysterious trio of clinic staffers to the feds and that this should help. He was told they would round them up for questioning within a few hours. But as of now, Al hadn't heard from Johnson or anyone else updating him about this.

"Just hang in there unc, and keep staying out of sight. The way I see it, we've got three things going for us. First, the girl riding with that gang who may or may not be on their side; second, those who may have seen the new plates put on their car enroute to the cities; and third, those medical staffers you overheard who hopefully can spill the beans on where this bunch is heading to do their dirty work."

While all this super strategy was going on, "Gal Sal" was tucked in the middle of two big sheiks. There was hardly any words spoken from the time all six of the desperadoes dashed off to make their official appointments with the underworld. The driver was still headed north but made sure his foot wasn't too heavy on the accelerator to catch the attention of any more patrol cars.

The eerie silence was broken only when Beck asked questions, which were promptly answered the way he wanted. Halfway between Cannon River and the turnoff to St. Paul, Beck, sitting next to the driver, turned his head, smiled as best he could with his sneering face and said: "Well done Salid," acknowledging her help.

The van they were riding in at this time, however, was not dark blue. Instead, it was a new red Ford Taurus with non-tinted windows. They seemed very pleased about this, knowing the police were on the lookout for an altogether different looking vehicle. As planned, one of their gang met them earlier on a side road near a corn field, switched vans with them, and drove off after carefully getting rid of their old plates. Everything seemed well organized, as Beck always demanded, to keep any possible pursuers guessing.

Meanwhile, guessing was exactly what Joe and Terry were doing in trying to catch up with the DNA researchers heard by Al deep within the clinic. Even though they had the names supplied by the PR head they couldn't locate them immediately. Not many staffers knew much about them since they joined the clinic only a few months ago, but already established a record of excellence in their specialties.

In talking with some of their colleagues about the researchers Namid, Hassmo and Lorena, authorities learned only that they were last seen in the clinic garage heading for their cars, each holding a brief case. But fortunately personnel files in the clinic's human resource department disclosed their home addresses and phone numbers. They also showed that each was a native of Pakistan.

The importance of rounding up this trio further increased once Johnson and Kavinsky heard the audio tape Benjamin gave them, as he tried to remain hidden from possible detection by any of the VIP visitors. It helped confirm that these professional medical scientists were indeed involved in trying to prevent authorities from finding a DNA match that would reveal the real Beck.

It was also necessary to visit each of the researcher homes to question them more extensively. Joe had his handcuffs ready, as well as Terry, and extra cops were on hand in unmarked cars. Upon entry to the homes, surprised women in robes were the first to greet them, along with barking and snarling dogs seemingly intent to bite on command.

Once ordered to be quiet, the dogs went obediently into their kennels. At least, thought Kavinsky, they weren't pit bulls or there could be more blood involved in this case. Upon showing their credentials and search warrants at each home, Joe and Terry asked to see the suspects. They were quickly summoned. However, each seemed more arrogant than scared by this sudden attack on what they considered to be their unquestionable and distinguished reputations.

Brief questioning didn't provide much information. To avoid loud interruptions by the women and dogs, the trio was led to the local police station for more detailed interrogation. Both Kavinsky and

Johnson conducted the questioning, realizing they had to get correct answers very quickly.

However, they encountered more than usual delays. Each suspect demanded an attorney while authorities were again reminded about possible international diplomatic protection. But not much could be argued about, once Al's tape was played back for all to hear. The suspect voices, although somewhat hushed, could be heard clearly, leaving no doubt to all in the interrogation room that the trio was plotting against the capture of Beck by obstructing valuable DNA evidence.

Before further questioning, however, their lawyers were backgrounded by authorities on the extreme importance of withholding any mention of what was happening from the media at this time. They were also advised that keeping the suspects in custody was strictly a matter of avoiding another possible terrorist incident.

"The less said about this, the better it will be for all of us," emphasized Joe. He had already urged his uncle Al not to alert the clinic and to encourage his more aggressive fellow reporters to temporarily avoid mentioning what was happening, at least until authorities could complete plans to capture the suspects being pursued before they can carry out their devilish scheme, whatever that might be.

Al winced at any attempt to squelch news, but went along with this scenario knowing it could mean saving lives. He also knew that the only reporter besides himself that might have any inside updated information would be his pal Smiley at the Press. After noodling this around for a while, however, Al concluded the best strategy would be to tactfully contact Smiley to talk about unrelated matters, and carefully feel him out if he or any of his cronies already had any inkling of Beck's pursuit.

Checking his watch, Benjamin knew Smiley would be at his "second office", just blocks away from the newspaper office, having a drink while reading the competitor newspaper in his favorite lunchtime hangout.

Al often teased Smiley about catching up on the news of the day by reading what the competitor paper wrote. And this time he was sure he would catch him doing it again.

When Al called, Smiley was on his cell phone immediately, and Al could tell he was already "juicing it up" again. Although Smiley was already slurring some words, Al was very careful not to give him any clues that he was trying to cut him off from a story lead, since Smiley, even with a few drinks, had a keen sense of detecting what was going on.

Knowing his area code may have come up on Smiley's phone monitor, Al pretended he was at the clinic for his annual checkup and that his old shoulder injury from the Army was acting up again. He purposely avoided mentioning his meeting with the clinic PR director, saying simply that he was calling to see if Smiley could join him for a Twins baseball game that coming weekend. Knowing his old friend was an avid Twins fan, he told him he was able to get a couple of complimentary tickets near the batter's box and was eager to give Smiley first dibs on these.

In a way, though, Al thought it unfortunate that Smiley jumped at the chance. Now he had the tough job of coming up with the tickets, especially such special ones desired by nearly everyone in town since the Twins were on a winning streak.

Al's heart skipped a beat, however, when Smiley asked if anything was happening down at the clinic. Smiley seemed satisfied, however, when Benjamin responded very casually, "Naw—everything's pretty quiet down here. You know, hardly anything ever happens in this quiet little town." Knowing that his paper and Smiley's were the only ones in the state with such broad readership circulations, Al added—"and pass that on to all your other news-scooping pals."

CHAPTER 23

Following this phone conversation Benjamin still was rather unsure that Smiley, with his super nose for news, was not wondering if Al was trying to cover up something. He knew Smiley was considered an exceptional reporter in digging out facts from fiction.

Meanwhile, the clinic researchers in custody remained very quiet. But with DEA and CIA advice, and support from their lawyers, they listened very carefully to how they might get some leniency from conspiracy charges against them.

As Johnson pointed out, if they help to lead to the capture of Beck they might be exonerated somewhat from severe criminal penalties. All three looked at each other and finally nodded compliance, with heads bowed as though accepting defeat—realizing that the tape, and Al witnessing their conspiracy, was too much to deny.

As part of his intense questioning, Johnson demanded to know where Beck and his gang were planning to spend that night, and what their plans were for the next day? Each glanced away from his stern direct stare, daring them to even look as though they were lying.

"At Amad's, Amad Turkos," replied Dr. Namid nervously. "I don't have his exact address."

"No…but I have," interrupted Joe, recalling hunting down Amad at his home in the Twin Cities' suburbs where he was hosting a crowd of Islamic friends.

The next question seemed more difficult for the nervous Namid.

"Did you find blood matching Beck's during your DNA research?"

Namid peered at his colleagues Hassmo and Lorena, as though wondering if they should go so far as to reveal their findings. Beads of sweat began forming on his forehead.

"Yes," said the Lorena answering for Namid. "There was a definite match."

"And whose was it?" asked Johnson anxiously.

Again, more hesitation. Finally, their companion Hassmo answered: "The little man with the limp."

Joe and Johnson smiled at one another, knowing they were right in their suspicion about Beck and his masquerade.

"The guy in the dress?" summed up Terry.

"Yes. That is the one. But he will kill us if he finds out we have told you this," said Lorena, her eyes pleading with authorities not to disclose their source of such information.

The trio told their inquisitors they were from wealthy families in an extremely conservative section of the world, and all were educated at American universities. They met the Beck drug ring during a fundamentalist Islamic convention and were deceived into thinking it could help enhance the Muslim religion and bring an end to all the ungodly like ways of liberal western civilization. Moreover, they felt the distribution of drugs into the U.S. would help bring about economic collapse and eventual destruction of its capitalistic system.

They also were warned that if they should ever show any disloyalties the consequence would be terrible humiliation, and even perhaps public execution.

"Wow," was all Joe could utter upon hearing this. "We'll help protect you. You can trust us to acknowledge your pleas for compassion. Surely you see the great inhumanity being done by this group."

Terry added, "No one will know your involvement and you will be under our protective custody at all times." With such assurance, the trio began to map out the strategy of the drug lord. Namid also assured them that the blood sample revealing Beck was still in a safe hiding place at the clinic.

"When can we obtain it?" asked Joe."As soon as you wish, but this must be done under absolute secrecy," Namid replied.

While all this was happening, Beck and his bunch, including Amad's girl friend, were pulling up in front of Amad's house. They were all ready to begin meeting with local drug kingpins in and around the Twin Cities area.

Both Kavinsky and Johnson realized that if they didn't catch up with them soon, Beck would be able to put into operation his desired expanded drug trafficking and money laundering network for probably much of the Upper Midwest.

"We can't let that happen, Terry," emphasized Kavinsky. "We only had several good leads to go on to begin with. One, replacing the license plates, didn't happen; and two, we really can't be very sure that Amad will stick to his word of not helping them. It looks like our 'Gal Sal' may still be our only one big hope."

"And where she'll lead us is another question. Perhaps it'll be to a place for terrorism. If we can get them all together at the same time this would be ideal," Terry said, putting his hand to his chin in trying to figure out some answers to this complex situation.

Both finally agreed that they should converge on Amad's house as soon as possible, and be strategically located in order to surprise and arrest the group without encountering great danger. They were sure each of the group was well armed—some perhaps even with explosives.

Rain and slippery roads slowed them down on the way to the house as the darkness of night rapidly closed in on them. As they got closer to their destination, Joe couldn't help but think this is a great time for spooks—then realized that's who they're after.

Amid such gloomy thoughts and surroundings, he was easily startled and somewhat frightened by the sudden loud ringing of Johnson's cell phone. Terry passed the phone to Joe after seeing on its monitor that the caller was Kavinsky's boss, chief Hermes.

"Joe, there's probably no use going to Amad's—he won't be there. We're not sure where he ran off to—who knows? maybe even Baghdad. He simply got away from us." Looking disappointed at Terry, Joe shrugged and said, "well, that's the second opportunity that's fallen through the cracks. If those dirtballs don't show up at the house we won't know where to look for them. God, Terry, they've broken away from us and can do their dirty work anywhere they wish."

"Yeah—we'll strike out without some more inside information."

Joe called chief Hermes back and requested that a couple of non-uniformed police in unmarked squad cars keep an eye on the home at the address he remembered when following Amad. In the meantime, he and Terry continued to head to the home in case Beck and his bunch show up. But, as predicted, Amad's house was dark and empty. The police patrol reported no activity whatsoever around the place. Joe and Terry, bewildered, stared at each other—wondering what to do next.

"Another missing person to report," Joe said shaking his head as though in despair.

"Yeah—but I hope he has better luck than our pal My Guy," Terry agreed, remembering that his undercover man My Guy was found hacked to death apparently by the same type of thugs Johnson and Kavinsky were pursuing.

"As you may recall, My Guy also was to be a whistle-blower for us until his cover was revealed. I'm sure Beck took great pleasure in doing away with him."

"Grotesque…but if we can find Amad soon enough we may be able to protect him," Kavinsky said shaking his head.

"I suspect it's too late, Joe. In fact, they may already have him buried under the cement floor of the basement."

"Well, what do we do—just sit here and wait?"

"I suggest we let our cops do that—they were told to round them up and bring them in if they show up at the house."

"Any idea where they may have gone otherwise?"

"Nope," Terry said with a shrug. "But I'm getting tired of all this, and a mite hungry…what say we find a place to chow down and discuss this in a more relaxed environment. I saw a ham-and-egg type restaurant about two blocks away."

After grabbing a couple of stools at the small restaurant counter, both ordered a cup of coffee, sandwich and piece of pie. They couldn't help but notice two highway patrolmen and truckers nearby, and figured this was a testimonial to good food.

Realizing it was still very important to speak softly—sometimes even whisper—about this case, Joe asked Terry's opinion regarding why it seemed the Beck gang was always one-step ahead of them,—and always able to disrupt their plans.

"Do you think there's an insider telling them our every move?"

"Could be. For instance, I always wondered whatever happened to Neil Cermak—your ex police chief, and if Doc Loring, the medical examiner, really drowned or safely escaped from us when we were all set to arrest them for their drug conspiracy."

Kavinsky noodled this around for a minute, then said: "you know, you may be on to something. Both knew Beck while dealing drugs with him,and Cermak, of course, was well aware of all the intricate workings of our police organization. For that matter, he could have easily sneaked Amad into our precinct. What's more, Loring was even found dealing with the Canadian and Bahamian traffickers."

"They never did find Loring's body did they?" asked Terry.

"Nope—I can't help but think he's still around. I heard he was a good swimmer who also worked out regularly at that ritzy private swim club where we found so many big shots connected with the local drug operations."

"But could either have much influence on Beck?" asked Johnson.

"He'd be more than happy to pay them very big bucks if they could wiggle him into the states again."

"So how do we know for sure this is happening, and better yet how can we stop it?"

"Our only chance would be from those we've caught so far—the guys at the clinic, including Amad—who we may never find—and that cloaked female who's still with Beck."

"You mean Sal—what's-her-face?"

"Exactly. The one with her face half hidden. She probably knows all the ins and outs of what's going on by now riding with those punks. We're down to three strikes, Terry. If we swing-and-miss this time we're out of the ball game.

"Besides, I'd love to get my hands on Cermak. He gave me so much trouble when I was working for him, it would give me great pleasure to put the cuffs on him," Kavinsky commented with a grin.

"What about Loring? Got any ideas how we might find out if he's still alive and getting in our way?"

"If we can get Cermak, I'm sure he'll show us how to get Loring. After all, there certainly was no love between them."

CHAPTER 24

As Terry was putting out an all-out points bulletin alert to the feds and Interpol to be on the lookout for Cermak, Beck and his bunch were almost laughing it up as they headed toward a rendezvous many miles from Amad's house.

"If they think Amad can help them, they'd better have a submarine," remarked Beck in his sneering way. All those around him, mostly body-guards peering out the windows of their new get-away van, laughed in unison as they thought of Amad on the bottom of Lake Calhoun with leg irons.

"No one knows my brother Maurice has some very nice accommodations near here. He hasn't been in touch with the cops—like Amad—and I'm sure you haven't been either Salid," said Beck placing his hand on her hand and squeezing it. She responded with a slight, but rather uneasy smile.

By this time uncle Al was finally safe at home. Following the tight security rules imposed in this case, he had assured his wife Kay that all was fine with his nephew and nothing bad was going on. He almost bit his lip, however, to avoid mentioning the sinister happenings at the clinic.

Al kept clicking his TV remote for updated news reports and reading the newspapers until Kay scolded him for skipping around her favorite programs. She once again threatened, in her teasing way, to go out and buy her own television set or hide the remote clicker if Al kept changing channels.

"What in the world are you looking for anyway?" asked his annoyed wife who said, "thank goodness we don't have twice as many networks as most of our neighbors do on cable or you'd be fooling with that remote all day."

Once convinced there were no news breaks at the clinic and that the only story of note was a drive-by shooting of a highway patrolman by an unknown assailant, Al finally turned off the TV and relaxed in his much-used recliner chair.

Just as he was about to doze off, however, Kay broke the silence with some more one-way conversation."By the way, the Post Office called again. Did you ever get to Joe about their wanting to talk to him?"

Grumpy for disturbing his attempt at sleeping, Al could only mutter: "Yes, for lord's sake. I told him at least twice, but he's been very busy—he said he'd be getting back to them as soon as possible. He's a big boy now, Kay, and has to handle such things himself."

"Well, it sounded important. The postal inspector also tried to contact Sarah—but you know how these young brides love to go shopping. He wanted to know if we could help contact them for a conference."

"Yeah—and Joe figures it's just a way for the Post Office to get involved with his detective work and help mess things up like the other feds are doing."

"My, what kind of work is he into now? That boy is always taking risks. I fear for his safety so often. I pray a rosary for him about once a day that the good Lord will look out for him."

"He has to do what he's told Kay. If the Post Office calls again just tell them he's busy right now and will be calling back as soon as possible."

Kay gave up, knowing she could go no further with this, and simply said with a shrug "whatever." She realized she did all she could in behalf of the Postal Service.

Sarah, however, wasn't shrugging off Joe's long absence from their bedside. Why hadn't he called at least when he wasn't going to be home for dinner? and why was he always so late? was it her fault? or was he distracted by some other woman who caught his eye? All these were among questions bothering and upsetting her lately.

And she couldn't help but recall how much her husband seemed attracted by that cute little Muslim girl who went out of her way to ask him to take that group photo at the mall.

It was getting late, and Sarah realized she had to get to bed since she was still employed as a buyer at Nieman Marcus and had to be at work early. She looked around their new home and wondered, with a sigh, when and if they both would have time in their busy schedules to ever remodel it like they planned, perhaps even with a baby room.

Once again Sarah tossed about in bed without anyone to snuggle up to. She and Joe had decided a few days earlier to buy a dog and she wished she had a nice little pet lying on the bed now as disturbing thoughts continued to keep her awake.

Sarah was only half awake when the ringing of the phone near the bed startled her so much she sat up like a puppet on a string. The voice on the other end brought comfort, however. It was Joe.

"Hi honey. Thought I'd check in. Sorry it's so late. This is real hush-hush stuff I'm on. I'm not suppose to say much, but wanted you to know everything's okay and wish that I was making love to you right now."

"When are you coming home?"

"Can't say, but I'm hoping it will be soon—maybe yet this week. This has turned out to be a complex mess. In the meantime, be sure not to say anything about what I might be doing, where I'm at or anything about me."

"And what am I suppose to be doing, Joe? Be a recluse and stay in the corner waiting for someone who I pretend doesn't exist?" his upset impatient wife responded. "No. But there's nothing I can do about that now. I'll make up for it, believe me. This is a crazy case and I'm dealing with crazy people honey. In the meantime, please be careful—I don't want anyone to bother you about this."

"What do you mean bother?…

"People who may want to know what I'm doing…even be a threat…the less said the better. Okay honey?"

"Okay Joe, I guess. Being married to a cop isn't always easy is it?"

"At least not now, damn it," said Joe "but don't forget I love you very, very much. So watch out—I can't wait to be back in bed with you."

Before he could click off his cell phone, Joe heard Sarah say "there's another thing I miss right now—a watch dog." The phone call from Kavinsky put Sarah into more of a sleeping mode, knowing all was well with her husband. In fact, she was nearly in dreamland when being suddenly awakened by a rainstorm.

The wind began blowing the window curtains, followed by loud claps of thunder so loud that Sarah got up to close the bedroom windows. She had difficulty fighting with the strong wind to prevent the rain from coming into the bedroom as she heard the curtains flapping about.

During all this disturbance she also heard something else…a strange sound came from the next room, as though near the kitchen. It could be that a kitchen curtain was fluttering. And then again it might be that the back door near the hallway leading to the kitchen was ajar caused by the sudden wind gusts. Whatever it was, it further alarmed Sarah—especially after hearing Joe's warning about being extra careful. She knew from the tone of his voice he seemed worried about her.

But living with a cop meant having some protection around you. Although Joe was no NRA activist, in his line of work he always recommended having a gun handy. He even had a name for the gun at home. He called it "Just in Case."

Sarah began searching for "Just in Case" immediately. She felt her heart speeding as she very quietly tried to find it without a flashlight. She thought for sure it was in the cabinet next to the bed, but it wasn't. She began thinking if some intruder was there she should open the bedroom window to jump out onto the roof. But before more panick set in, she suddenly remembered Joe tucking the gun into the top drawer of the bedroom dresser.

Sarah felt embarrassed about all this, knowing she was probably over-reacting as she groped for the pistol. What upset her even more was that she wasn't sure if the gun was even loaded. Knowing Joe, he was always very safety-first conscious—even lecturing to kids about not handling a loaded gun. And then again, if it wasn't loaded, where would she find the bullets?

The more nervous she became, the more the sounds from the kitchen seemed to be getting closer. Oh God, she thought, where is that gun! Just then, as if the Almighty heard her, her fingers felt what seemed to be a gun butt. Seizing it, she yanked it from the overstuffed dresser drawer and then turned on the bedroom lights to see if it was loaded.

But before she could examine it, she heard the kitchen door slam, as though someone was leaving or entering. Nervously peeking into the kitchen while holding the gun, as if ready to shoot, she noticed the kitchen door was slightly opened. At first, this lessened her fears since she may have forgotten to close it. But instead of feeling safe, Sarah recalled that she had made it a special point to carefully lock and latch each door of the house before going to bed. There was no way the door could have been opened except by someone tampering with it.

She quickly slammed the door shut and locked it, but while trying to put the latch back on it fell to the floor. Someone may have broken it, she thought. Extra cautious, she also rolled down the window awning as though making doubly sure no-one could ever get an arm through the window to open or even peek through it.

Sarah inwardly scolded herself for probably being a "fraidy cat", however. That's what her sister Susan used to call her to shame her if she got scared when they were kids. As she turned away to return to the bedroom, though, she suddenly realized she wasn't such a "fraidy cat" after all. She became a downright coward.

On the top of the cabinet-island, in the middle of the kitchen, appeared to be a note. It was just lying there with a tab of tape holding it in place. She knew it wasn't there before going to bed. As she nervously and curiously approached the small piece of paper, she could see some bold red lettering on it.

Although she left her glasses in the bedroom, it was obvious to Sarah that whoever wrote it was in one hell of a big hurry, perhaps fleeing when she turned on the bedroom lights. But on closer inspection, what really frightened her mostly was that the words were scribbled in blood.

Sarah let out a muffled scream when seeing the still wet blood. Recalling her police husband's warning about never leaving prints on anything that may be evidence, she was extra careful not to touch the dirty, ragged note paper while squinting to make sure she was reading each word correctly.

As she feared, it was a warning. It read: *TELL YOUR HUSBAND TO LAY OFF THE BECK CASE. IF HE DOESN'T—HE'LL HAVE A DEAD WIFE.*

CHAPTER 25

All this was happening while Kavinsky was deep in thought, trying to determine the next move to catch up to the Beck bunch at a meeting with his "comrades in arms" at the clinic. When his cell phone jingled, next to the pistol on his belt, he thought for a moment that it may be a nuisance call from a telemarketer or even that darn annoying Post Office until noticing the phone number was from home.

Sarah could hardly talk she was so shaken and on the verge of tears. In fact, Joe had to ask her to twice repeat what she was trying to say. When he finally understood, he excused himself from the meeting and went to a private room to try to listen more intently and calm her down.

Joe promised he would call his precinct immediately and have an inspector come to the house. The blood may help with DNA research. He thanked her for not leaving her fingerprints on the note. He also assured Sarah he would fly up to the Twin Cities airport on the next available flight to be with her. In the meantime, he suggested that she be extremely careful, and to check the phone directory to see where watchdogs are available. He suggested calling the police canine department.

On the brief flight home, Joe spent most of the time pondering over how the intruder got into the house. He recalled spending lots of time, effort and money putting special locks on each door along with latches. It almost looked like an inside job. He scoffed at the thought, however, since Sarah was the only one at home at the time.

That's it! Allowing his detective mind to take over, Joe figured that perhaps someone was in the house prior to that time. Perhaps a plumber, carpenter—whoever. If so, maybe he—or she—was able to tamper with the lock and latch in preparation for breaking into the house that night.

He was almost certain that the intent was to scare his wife so much that she would insist on having him stop meddling with this Beck pursuit. But he knew the risk was very apparent now, and that the next time the intruder might be an assailant who wouldn't hesitate to murder Sarah.

Sarah knew this, too, and lost no time in trying to find a recommended attack dog that could sniff out anyone trying to break into their beloved wedding nest. The policeman who came to the house was from a canine trainer and "loaned" her one of their most alert, and what might be regarded at first as a possible ferocious, guard dogs—appropriately a full grown and very friendly looking German Shepherd.

When introduced to this large pointy-nose animal waging its tail, Sarah was a bit taken back. "Will it bite me if I try to pet it?" she asked timidly.

"Of course not, Stella is a very gentle, well-trained police dog," the trainer assured.

"Stella?" Sarah said, surprised by such a sissy name for such a tough-looking animal.

"Yeah—She was a pet a few years ago for some little girls who named her. When the family moved to the West Coast the parents decided to donate her to the police. Almost broke their hearts—and Stella's too.

"But don't let her kid you—she can be mean when she has to. She'll make up to you and your husband right away but, like this breed, she'll be very protective of her masters. She's trained to bark, snarl and scare the hell out of anyone trying to enter the house unless you tell her not to. Just say no—and she'll back off."

The trainer left after carefully taking the threatening note with its blood stains and other evidence with him to the station for further examination.

Stella was put to the test a few hours later, when Joe put a key in the door to be welcomed home. About the only welcome he received, however, was loud, vicious growling and barking on the other side of the door. He was positive no one in their right mind would want to venture further. However, he figured anyone who may want to break in may not possess a "right mind."

A loud "no" was heard from inside, and the dog quickly shut up.

Following much hugging and kissing while Stella closely looked on with her tail wagging again, Joe put his hand out to scratch Stella's ears. The dog immediately changed from being gentle to snarling. "No" again was the command from Sarah, and Stella then nuzzled up to Joe wagging its tail and waiting for more petting.

"Boy, you've already trained him well honey," Joe said approvingly, "either that or she's just a big teddy bear."

"I hope not. The real test will be if someone tries breaking in here again."

Telling Joe about her ordeal, she included mentioning searching for his gun and using it to defend herself if needed. She was surprised, however, to hear that it wasn't loaded.

"The bullets are in the same cabinet, in a container in back of the gun. Sorry I didn't make that clear. I don't like to have a loaded weapon in the house. I've seen too many accidents with them."

"But Joe, I could've been killed thinking I could keep the intruder away from me with that empty weapon," Sarah argued. "I know. And believe me from now on it will be ready for your pretty trigger finger. Hopefully, you'll never get into that situation again and that old Stella here will make sure you're safe," he said winking at the big beast playfully sharpening his teeth on a rubber bone next to Kavinsky's feet.

While scratching the dog's ears, the phone rang. Both Joe and Sarah were shocked to hear the crime lab director report. "Joe, that blood on the note paper matches Amad's. The DNA's the same. Somehow someone kept a little spilled blood and sent it to you as a terrible warning."

Kavinsky was greatly upset, but not too surprised. Although expecting it might be from a goat or other animal, he figured it was possible that it might match up with some of Beck's mob. But regardless, the researchers at the clinic already had all of the DNA proof needed regarding Beck's involvement.

The lab boss added, "We also found some prints on the note paper. But the person they may match up with—we don't know."

"Sounds interesting. Could you run them through your computer to find out if there's any possible match from suspects we finger printed over the past two years?" Joe asked.

"Boy, that's a big order Joe," exclaimed the director. "That takes at least a week or so, and then we might be skipping some."

"That's okay. I'm sure chief Hermes will approve. Let's give it a try and see what we come up with." With that, Kavinsky clicked off his phone and concentrated more on his voluptuous bride. But just as he and Sarah were about to hit the sheets there was another cute little jingle from his cell phone as though the caller intentionally meant to interrupt their love making.

No one seemed to be on the other end of the phone, not even a telemarketer. Usually there would be some sort of voice, asking for either the husband or wife if it was a sales call. But there was nothing on the caller-ID.

However, as Joe was about to hang up and get on with what he really loved doing, a tiny voice—almost a whisper—could finally be heard on the phone. It sounded like the voice of a young woman. But he had to press his ear very close to the phone to know what she was trying to say.

At first he thought it might be a sex pervert on the line, since all he could hear was breathing. Almost like someone trying to catch their breath. Then, very softly, in between nervous breathing, came a voice Joe remembered. It was Salid, the one they call Sally...the girl who was granted a plea bargain and willing to be the DEA's undercover in the Beck mess.

"Mr. Kavinsky, it is I Salid Ashid. I must talk fast and very silently. I am with Mr. Beck. He will kill me like he has Amad if he knows what I'm doing. I wish to help you and gain my freedom."

"Where are you at?" asked Joe lowering his voice also as if to add to the secrecy of the call. "I do not know for sure. But it is with Mr. Beck's relative Maurice outside the cities. I can only tell you now that we will be at the mall in two days to meet with others. Beck is a terrible man. I want nothing to do with him. You must believe me."

"How can I contact you to protect you?"

"Do not try—they must never know I made this call. I must go now."

As Joe put down the phone, his wife was looking intently at him, studying his every move and expression.

"Was that your girl friend again?" she asked with a pretended frown. "Does she usually call you at bedtime, and when you're alone?"

Joe looked at Sarah with a sheepish grin. "You know better than that. This was all business Sarah...business I can't even talk about with you. Besides, where did I leave off with our love affair?" Sarah giggled as Joe eagerly crawled over to her side tossing the bed sheets aside.

As they re-snuggled up for some more deep, passionate love, Joe however couldn't keep from thinking at times about the woman who called—he knew she must be desperate to get away from Beck to risk making that call, and to prove she was still keeping her promise of helping to capture him.

But the many different local and federal authorities impatiently wanting Beck were still puzzled over how best to round him up after hearing Joe's report about the surprised phone call. It left no evidence where it originated or any other way to trace the source.

In a meeting the next day with a CIA agent, Kavinsky was told, "We've searched everywhere, Joe, but can't find a Maurice Beck in the entire metro or suburban areas. In fact, we've checked every directory, from city and suburb phone books to those listing business people and professionals, even doctors, lawyers and used car salesmen.

"We're right back where we started—ground zero. Hell, we're not even sure what mall that woman was talking about for that matter. There must be umpteen malls in the metro and suburban areas."

Kavinsky was quick to interrupt. "I know this much, though, there's only one she's talking about—the giant megamall where I first met her."

"You know that for sure?"

"I'd bet my life on it—but then again I almost lost my life there," he said with a frown.

The agent reminded Kavinsky that there are literally thousands of people, all types and ages, passing through the doors of the super mall every day.

'There's no way we could possibly identify each one, especially any who wish to be disguised."

"There may be one way," Joe interrupted as though a light bulb went off in his head.

"There's always Pete the piano player."

CHAPTER 26

While all this was going on, thousands of miles away lots of things were also happening off a popular shore in Bermuda. What looked like a fishing contest was taking place involving crews of men with nets and hooks casting into the deep, rough Atlantic ocean.

While the fishermen in their small seaworthy crafts fought the splashing waves around the rocky reefs, large vessels were nearby to come to their help if necessary. Some were marked Police and others Postal Service.

The occupants of the police vessels all wore uniforms, including official badges and caps. One, in full regalia, although outdated, looked familiar. In fact, he stood out from the others giving orders and pointing to places for the searchers to look.

There would be no question in the minds of many Twin Citians, that this indeed was Neil Cermak, the former St. Paul police chief who had fled arrest months ago for collaborating with drug trafficking in the Twin Cities, the Bahamas and elsewhere.

Cermak fit in perfectly. He loved wearing police caps and looking important. He probably had on some of his old police clothing. But Minnesota and the Bahamas were a long ways from the Bermuda islands, which raised the questions: why was he there? and how did he escape the many authorities searching for him all this time?

Having been in close touch with Zack Crimmons during his reign of drug trafficking and prior to Crimmons' drowning, Cermak was one of the few who knew Zack's latest address and where he may have unloaded some of the payoffs he received

Soon after Cermak escaped the law, which he so often misrepresented, he carefully researched the location of Zack after fleeing to Colombia to be protected by his fellow drug thugs. With their help, Cermak figured Bermuda was where Zack tossed his ill-gotten money, along with himself, into the sea. Who knows, maybe even Zack was able to rise again, Cermak scoffed thinking about his old criminal pal.

It was easy for Cermak to obtain a job with the Bermuda police by simply falsifying his records and showing his police academy records. But he had no idea that his buddy-in-crime, Dr. Loring, the medical examiner who also falsified records—dealing with murder he would often keep secret—was also on the hunt for this water-soaked treasure. Loring had been considered dead, with his obituary even posted in the Twin Cities papers. After all, his last words as he was going down in the freezing waters of Lake Calhoun in Minneapolis were: "I can't swim! I can't swim!" What's more, Kavinsky even saw this mad doctor sink in the lake when he tried to capture him. To be saved, however, Loring would have had to cling closely onto the bottom of the diving platform where the cops stood and be able to suck in air coming through the wooden floor beams. Since everyone departed from the platform shortly after presuming the doctor was drowned, it was still possible for him to find a way to survive—perhaps with the help of some innocent snowmobile driver who was passing by and noticed Loring, an expert swimmer at a St. Paul exercise club, waiving to be taken safely back to shore.

Whatever the reason, Cermak and Loring were still alive and up to their old evil tricks, although no longer in the minds of police or federal agents who believe both were history and, thankfully, unable to ever re-surface again.

But the ever-persistent Cermak was very much determined to personally check into the possibility of any of Zack's money still floating on top of the ocean. What brought him to this isolated reef next to the Bermuda's capital was a report that one of the natives spotted some bills around a spot too deep for even an Olympic swimmer or snorkeling instructor.

Loring on the other hand, was pursuing the money as a passenger on the cabin cruiser that Crimmons jumped from along with his cache of U.S. and foreign bills. He had already talked with the ship's captain who witnessed Sarah's dad floundering futilely in the ocean's turbulent waters.

Unlike the evildoers Joe was pursung, Cermak and Loring needed no disguise. After all, there was no APB bulletin put out on them, thanks to Cermak's knowledge of how to sabotage and stop any notices given to the Interpol police.

Kavinsky, of course, seldom thought about these guys, but when he did he couldn't help but wonder if they indeed were still causing crime. When he did think of Cermak he also wondered about Paulson, who was assigned as Joe's partner by the former chief and who often got in his way. But Paulson turned out to be a good guy, as far as Joe could determine. When he thought of doc Loring, however, his mind conjured up that frightened, dreadful face of the doctor's screaming as he slowly sunk into the murky Twin Cities lake. But Joe often wondered if he wasn't faking it.

But right now Kavinsky was concentrating all of his thoughts and efforts into how best to catch up to that beast of all beasts-Beck. Things were much too quiet for Joe's energetic, suspicious police instincts. From experience, he knew that this may very well be the calm before the storm.

He felt that too much reliance was being put on the cooperation of "gal Sal", who may be hard pressed just to survive. While figuring out who to trust and who not to, Kavinsky's cell phone rang so loud that several feds around him almost reached for their guns. They kidded him to put a pretty tune on his cell phone instead.

"Relax guys, it's just another cop," Joe grinned placing the phone to his ear.

"Joe, it's me—Dave Paulson. I'm shocked to hear that my partner may be dead. God, those guys mean business. If it's any help, I checked over Amad's old email messages that may assist us in getting Beck."

"Are there any indicating where he might be now?"

"None that I can see, but I'm still going over some. Geez, this guy was on the buddy list of zillions. Some of the writing's in strange language, looks a little like Islamic scribbling."

"Probably so. Be sure to buzz me again Dave if you get anything leading us to him."

Joe took time for a quick deep breath after talking with Paulson and then got back to thinking how to out-maneuver Beck's next move. As he recalled, "Sally" had whispered over the phone that the group will eventually be at the super mall.

"We have to be one-step ahead of this guy," exclaimed Kavinsky in updating Johnson.

"Yeah—maybe even two. You mentioned someone named Pete—how the hell does he fit into this Joe?"

"He's the piano player at the mall—I've known him for years. His name is really Pietro—a good Italian lad who's a whiz on the keyboard. And you should hear him sing—wow! It's a shame they make him stick strictly to the keys. But he also gets to hawk his audio tapes and pass out his calling cards around the piano."

"So how does this relate to Beck?" asked the frowning DEA agent.

"A signal, Terry…a signal. Get it?"

"The only signal I'm receiving Joe is that you need a break from this mess. It's obviously interfering with your brain signals. How can your piano player be of any help to us?"

"He already has been," replied Kavinsky, who then related the time Pete signaled Joe that Salid was in the mall by playing a special tune pre-arranged by Joe who provided a rough sketch of her.

"This isn't something you can pass off with a song, Joe," warned Terry, trying to be creative himself.

"We could try at least…if all else fails."

"Whatever"…Terry agreed indifferently, mostly to go on with more serious matters.

"But I think we should try to get information from that list your buddy Paulson has of Amad's e-mail. We'd better assign an agent to work with Dave to see what if any leads we can obtain."

"My uncle Al could help, he's a great snoop and may be able to pick out something special, beyond what one of your agent's can. They may be too new to this case."

"But he's a reporter, Joe. For God's sake we don't need any press attention on this now."

"He's also a key to keeping this secret. I know him real well. Al is capable of steering other reporters away. He knows how they think, what interests them most and all kinds of other things that their editors are looking for. With that in mind, he can use his special strategy to keep them away."

Joe added, "he also knows how important this operation is to all of us. If this bunch has its way there could even be another September 11 incident—only much sooner."

"Where's he at?" inquired Johnson. "You may be a bit biased, but I'll buy what you're selling."

"He's probably back at his news desk, just waiting to hear from us as he turns out stories at his word-processor."

To make an even additional case for using Benjamin, Kavinsky added, "Al knows some of the characters in this scenario Terry. He could probably even spot Sally if he saw her."

"Sounds like you've been doing some talking to your uncle," responded Johnson, as a reminder to Kavinsky that he was supposed to keep this operation as private as possible.

"I'm guilty, but I must admit that when it comes to uncle Al's great abilities in uncovering a story—or covering one up and squelching it—no one can top him."

Kavinsky won the argument. After further discussion, Terry became convinced that Benjamin could indeed be helpful to Paulson in checking out suspicious contacts and written messages to the late Amad. One of the most convincing factors was that Al had a very low profile in this case—after all he spent most of his time hiding, as his nephew ordered.

Paulson, however, still wasn't too sure he wanted Joe's uncle to be so much involved. Although Joe seemed friendlier with Paulson since he helped with arresting some of the drug smugglers months ago, Dave still sensed Kavinsky's dislike and distrust. Plus, he couldn't help but wonder if Benjamin felt the same way since Joe and his uncle work so closely together at times.

Despite these feelings, Paulson tried contacting Benjamin as soon as he was told to do so by chief Hermes. All he got was a busy signal, however. If Al had a voice mail on his phone he could at least leave a message for him to call back. But knowing Joe's uncle, he realized he wouldn't spend any money on such extras. Paulson's only alternative was to call Benjamin's home in hope that his wife Kay would let her husband know he wanted to hear from him.

But Paulson gave up reaching Al, and was all set to turn out his desk light at the precinct and go home when a call came from Benjamin, who spoke so softly Paulson could hardly hear him. Seems that Al was doing so much hiding and whispering lately he didn't know when to speak up. He just wanted to check in. Paulson got his message across, however, and Al agreed to meet with him at the precinct early the next morning.

Benjamin shook off any thoughts of working very long with Paulson. He figured that any notes or e-mails Amad may have received relating in any way to Beck or drug smuggling, or anything tied-in with this, would take only a brief time to research.

It became apparent that Amad was considered quite low on Beck's hierarchy of henchmen, having been planted in the police precinct perhaps mostly by Cermak before the former police chief "disappeared."

In fact, he was so low on this totem pole, guessed Al, that Beck lost no time in getting rid of Amad upon questioning his loyalty.

Benjamin kept this in mind when looking over Paulson's shoulder as Amad's communications records were studied. His constant presence and occasional nose blowing were annoying to Paulson, who finally asked Al to grab a nearby chair and sit down. "I'm giving you all I have on my ex-partner, Al. It's better to read this sitting down than standing up. Keep in mind, though, that Amad was from the Mideast and his communications from others was sometimes in a very different language."

"I'll admit, I have a difficult time even reading some English when it's in Amad's handwriting," said Al.

"It'll be easier when we check out his electronic mail. And don't forget his computer recycle bin. He may have tried to delete some of the secret stuff, not knowing that it still could be filed in that bin on his computer," noted Paulson.

"You mean he didn't use the old shredding machine, like so many of our CEO's and accountants use today so shareholders can't learn the truth about their corporations' financial trickery?' commented Benjamin rather jokingly.

Paulson grinned along with Benjamin, knowing how some top shady business leaders can hide from the law by destroying evidence. But they quickly returned to the business of scrutinizing Amad's files and how he hid from authorities.

Amad was well organized, unlike many of the detectives who had sketchy little messages or Post-it Notes hanging around their desks or walls to remind them of assignments and schedules. One file in particular captured the attention of Al. It was marked confidential. However, it was also tightly locked…with no key in sight.

Noticing Benjamin's frustration at not being able to open the file cabinet, and the noise he was making shaking it, Paulson came quickly to his assistance with a large crow bar and wire cutter.

"We're always ready for emergencies around here Al," boasted Paulson

"My God, how often do you have to do this. I thought cops had everything at their fingertips." Benjamin responded.

"You thought wrong Al…it's reporters who have that," teased Paulson as he grunted and strained in breaking the lock away from the file drawer.

The first file both noticed was labeled "Executive". It stood out from the others in both size and color. The entire folder was a mixture of garish blue and yellow with an off-green label, much different than the plain tan files in the cabinet.

"Let's hope what's in here is more attractive than its container," remarked Al.

Upon removing the file from the cabinet and placing it on their desk for close inspection, both began carefully removing the numerous ingredients.

"Holy smokes Dave!" was Benjamin's first utterance. "Look at some of the names on these papers. Amad must have had the goods on an awesome collection of key influential people around this town."

Paulson immediately focused on Al's files to see if he recognized anyone listed. He stood up and looked over Al's shoulders at the papers being removed from the file, making sure he wasn't missing anything.

"You're right Al. There's some names here that would make great headlines on your newspaper scandal pages."

"Yeah, and that's why I'm here—to try to avoid that…at least until everything is thoroughly checked to see if Amad isn't out to do these guys in. But with all the corporate lies and money-mishandling going on, we might indeed be on to something very big Dave."

The information in this file, as well as others less sensational, was of such interest to both of the curious men that they spent the next several hours reading each of the many pages and taking notes.

"Boy, some of these auditors were really off the mark. Lots of conspiracy with the top corporate leaders," mumbled Paulson as Benjamin kept jotting down comments scribbled along the margins of nearly every page by Amad without taking time to talk.

Both noted that in nearly every case, there was a connection with drug trafficking in one form or another. It was quite obvious that those mentioned were either tied in with Beck or with someone affiliated with the drug lord.

"Geez—what guts for Amad to be coordinating this right here at our station—under our very nose," Paulson said sighing.

"On the other hand, this may have been an ideal place for him to be doing it," Al noted.

"After all, who would have suspected this—it was so risky, so bold hardly anyone ever would think he could get away with it."

"You're right," said Paulson stroking his beard and shaking his head in thought, "and worst yet he was right in the midst of hearing what the police were planning—and our attempts to stop it and catch the bad guys, including Beck."

With that, Paulson went to the water cooler in a corner near the administration department to take a break, as though in deep thought and not wanting to be interrupted. He seemed perplexed over how all this could have happened on his watch. Meanwhile, Benjamin, with his nose for news, couldn't help but continue to shuffle through the very interesting and confidential reports he found in the file.

Al was suddenly stopped in his tracks, however, by what he saw toward the end of his search. A couple of names hit him like the proverbial ton of bricks. Infact, he had to look twice to make sure of what he thought he had seen. Yes, there they were: the names of Cermak and Loring.

What's more, there were no asterisks or other marks after the names indicating they were missing or dead. There were lots of footnotes, though, and as Benjamin read further it was quite apparent that these guys were very much alive and probably doing very well.

Al almost instinctively reached for his cell phone, without even thinking of alerting Paulson. He clicked onto his nephew's numbers but just heard a busy signal since Joe was on his phone trying to reach Al at the same time regarding Amad's writing. He also wondered how the hell Amad ever got his job without being able to communicate better. Although Amad claimed to be from Pakistan, his scribbling looked like Greek.

After several attempts, Al was greatly relieved when his next call finally got through to Joe.

"Joey, this is your uncle—guess what?"

"For God's sake unc, this is no time for games," yelled Kavinsky busy with Terry in searching for Beck.

"Chief Cermak and doc Loring are still with us."

"Huh?" was all the surprised Kavinsky could utter.

"It's true. Amad has it all down in his notes on file at the precinct."

"Does he know where they're at?"

"I haven't gotten that far in the file yet. But I should have more details for you within the hour."

"But uncle Al, I saw Loring drowning."

"Yeah, but did they find the body?"

"No—but hopefully they will. There's still some ice on the lake. It takes time to do that. A big body with probably lots of attachments, like guns, most likely is on the bottom of that lake—and won't be rising for some time. It's like Sarah's dad, the weight would pull him down in the water and keep him there."

His uncle interrupted, "believe me Joe, he's back on land and probably figuring out his next evil move. As for Cermak, Amad had the goods on him, too. I may even be able to tell you where he's hanging out after I'm finished reviewing Amad's correspondence."

"Just be careful not to tell anyone else first. And also, if you can do it, don't tell your associate Paulson about it," cautioned Joe.

"He's not even around, Joe. I can tuck this part of the file in my coat without anyone knowing. But why not Paulson?"

"Dunno—I still wonder where he stands in all this. The less said the better at this stage. However, I'll be turning this information over to my DEA partner Johnson. I'm sure he'll also be interested in anything else you come up with from those files—big shots or little shots."

"I'm beginning to think greed is behind it all, Joe. You know: the more you have, the more you want. This must be a reason why so many of the big guys are running off with millions and leaving so many others laid off with nowhere to turn."

"Greed's the carrot, unc, but drugs are often the driving force," his nephew summed up.

"Yeah, and as the slogan says: 'Drugs beget Terrorism.'"

"Well—now that we've got that all figured out let's go get those rascals unc," said Joe. "You do your thing and I'll do mine. And, hopefully, the DEA will do their's—on Cermak and Loring. But right now mine is trying to get to the little lady who seems to know every step Beck is taking—and where and what it's going to lead to."

Kavinsky was referring, of course, to Salid and her reference to the mall as being a possible target during her call to Joe the other night. It would make things far less complicated if he could simply call her back on his cell phone, like nearly everyone else seemingly involved in this weird telecommunications scenario. But unfortunately nothing came up on his caller-ID to indicate where she's calling from.

Performing the ordinary security measures, such as alerting mall police or calling out the sheriff or National Guard couldn't be done since this would stir up everyone, especially the news media. These thoughts led Joe right back again to thinking about Salid. His crime lab still had her sketch on file and he was certain he could get it into the hands of Pete when, and if, his piano-playing pal was still playing his tunes at the mall.

This required a call to Pete's residence, which wasn't easy since he was a bachelor and flitted around a little from apartment to apartment, condo to condo. He wasn't an employee of a company, nor was he associated with any organization. At night, you may as well forget trying to contact him—Pete was so much in demand doing his piano gigs that he might be found anywhere, from a cabaret pounding out Jazz or at a wedding reception playing a romantic tune for the dancing bride-and-groom.

Fortunately, Joe still had Pete's calling-card in his pocket, the one promoting his project-to-project performance availability. Also printed on it were his cell-phone, fax and website numbers. But it was like flipping a coin to see what one Pete would be more apt to answer. Joe ended up trying all—but without any luck.

The only other way was to call the mall—perhaps someone there, like the music coordinator, would know his schedules. But, unfortunately, the coordinator was on vacation for a couple of weeks. The only thing left for Joe was to drive up to the Twin Cities and try to catch Pete at the mall's piano.

His trip, however, paid off. He could almost hear the swinging piano-playing of Pete before opening the big mall front doors. This guy's really good—it's why some call him maestro, Joe figured, as he began whistling to the tune being played while passing by the same big barricade planters where he nearly swallowed poison.

With his hands in his pocket, Joe felt the paper sketch he picked up at the precinct on his way to the mall. He took it out briefly to see if it still looked like Salid. It did—almost an exact likeness in fact. He hoped, however, that she didn't do anything to change her appearance.

Walking around the department leading to the piano next to the up-escalator, and still humming softly to the upbeat playing of Pete, he surprisingly spotted his lovely wife studying a pair of shoes on sale.

"Boo!" said Joe, startling Sarah, while also tapping her on the shoulders as she was busy shoe gazing. "I really like that pair—it would go with your beautiful eyes."

"Silly—you've been gone so long you hardly know the color of my eyes," responded the startled Sarah. I didn't know you were coming home today Joe—and what in the world are you doing in this place after going through that terrible incident you ran into here recently?"

"You mean with the planter flowers and that bad coffee?"

"You know what I mean. I've been waiting to hear from you. I thought you were still down at the clinic checking things out."

"That didn't stop you from shopping though," grinned Joe trying to placate the situation. Sarah frowned instead of grinning back. Joe was quickly thinking of another way to defend his absence when he noticed the piano playing stopped.

"Look honey, I'm sort of on duty now. I've got to catch the piano player before he leaves."

"The piano player! Why—has he hit some bad notes or something?" Sarah said sarcastically with her hands on her hips.

"Nope, never—he's always on the right keys."

"Then what's the big deal about the piano player?" asked Sarah putting Joe more on the defense.

"I—I just want to show him something," explained a somewhat nervous and impatient Kavinsky, not wanting to tell Sarah too much about what's going on.

"I just want to show him a picture."

"A picture of what" Sarah inquired almost taking pleasure in seeing her husband squirm.

"Of a girl—you don't know her," said Joe who immediately was sorry he said such a thing and realized he was digging himself further into a very awkward situation.

"Let's see her," was Sarah's quick command.

"Aw, you don't want to see it, it's all crumpled up in my pocket."

Joe was feeling more like an idiot as this conversation went on.

"Joe—let me see it. It isn't of that sweet little thing who calls you at night?"

"Now honey, you knew that was on business—and this is on business too—police business. But I can't discuss it right now," he said trying to explain.

"Okay—but it's a good thing I'm a trusting wife. Go ahead with your girl-watching. But I'm ready to go home to our bed—alone. Call me when you have the chance," snapped Sarah as she turned and walked irritated toward the mall exit.

Kavinsky was left scratching his head. He figured at first that he'd better buy those cute little shoes she was looking at to make amends. But then he realized why he came to the mall in the first place. He looked around quickly and luckily caught the pianist still stuffing his sheet music into his brief case ready to call it a night.

"Before you put the lid down on that baby grand Pete please take another look at the sketch of this young lady we still want to question," Joe requested.

"But Joe we just went through this not long ago. You mean you haven't caught her yet?"

"We will—hopefully with your help. We have good information that she'll be coming to the mall with a group of others—who we don't know. One of them, however, is the person the U.S. government has been after for many years. He's in disguise, but I'm pretty certain our lady friend will still be looking like this sketch."

"Do other cops know about this? I'm surely not the only one you're counting on to help snag her."

"This is a highly secretive operation, Pete. Yes, some security will be at the other entrances also with the sketch. But you and I have actually seen her and most likely can more readily spot her."

"But Joe are you the only one that will know my piano signal?"

"No—the others will, too. Like me, they're to immediately contact you with this pager beeper I'll be giving to you to find out where you've seen her and where her group may be heading."

As Joe passed on the special beeper to Pete, he thought of another important point. "And for God's sake Pete don't play that silly kid's tune again—you know, the 'Better Watch Out for Santa Claus' one. Besides, they may be on to it by now."

"What do you want me to play?"

"I dunno—something more appropriate and up-to-date; yet a song that'll let us know you've got 'em in your sights."

Pete snapped his fingers as though a brilliant idea hit him. "I know—how about "I've got You—I've got you under my skin."? Do you remember that old one?"

Joe paused to consider this and then with a smile said, "By George I think you've got it. I'll let the others know. In the meantime, you'd better be practicing that in private."

CHAPTER 27

❁

As Joe left the store he glanced again at those cute shoes that Sarah was gazing at so fondly. The temptation was too much. Even though they weren't on sale he dugged deep, handed over many bills, and tucked them under his arm.

As he made his way out the door, and past those notorious big planters, he was whistling again—only this time the tune was: "I've Got You Under My Skin". On his way home he couldn't help but think of making up for some of the love and passion he had to forsake with Sarah during his hunt for the evil ones.

Upon arriving, he embraced his wife and for a moment thought how great it would be to also have some kids running up to hug you. Right now, however, all of his love was focused on Sarah, with nothing to spare for anyone else.

Since it was late they headed up to their cozy little bedroom where Joe found time in between love-making to show Sarah the new shoes he bought for her.

His thoughtfulness paid off in many ways. She forgot all about being peeved over Joe's tardiness and was most cooperative in the passion she bestowed. Who knows, thought, Joe, maybe this also could already be the start of having some huggable kids.

But all this bliss came to a loud halt as once again the phone rang.

Oh God, not now, murmured Kavinsky. His worst fear was realized, however. Sarah got to the phone first and heard what she didn't want to hear: "Hello is Mr. Kavinsky there?." It was a young lady's voice—the same one that interrupted their intimate love affair in the past.

Sarah was almost tempted to yell "hell no" and hang up. But instead angrily thrust the phone into Joe's hands and said "your girl friend again."

Kavinsky began sweating. All this was getting to be too much even for him. But the conversation was extremely brief. He simply heard, in almost a whisper, the word "tomorrow."

"What about tomorrow?" shot back Joe.

"Tomorrow the mall—Be there. Can't talk anymore. Just be there."

That was the extent of the phone talk. Joe still held the phone as Sarah broke the quiet by saying: "what's she want now—besides your love?"

Explaining this awkward situation wasn't easy, especially since most of it was still secret, but considering her husband's type of work Sarah was more than understanding. She also knew this meant that he had to get up bright and early the next morning, long before the stores open, to go over plans with his cohorts to catch Beck—so their love making beneath the sheets had to be brief.

Before he could catch any sleep, however, Joe first had to phone his team of security people to be on guard at their assigned stations for the mall opening and be prepared for the bad guys, no matter what direction they may come from. After that, he turned out the lights and gave Sarah a very long and passionate kiss goodnight. She cuddled up even closer to make love knowing that her man could indeed be trusted.

While preparing to go on his manhunt again the following morning and attend the planning meeting, Kavinsky still felt guilty about not telling Sarah what was going on with him and that mystery female night caller.

Sarah arose from bed still with a smile on her face as he was packing his gun into his shoulder holster. As a young wife protective of her husband, she asked him how dangerous the day was going to be for him. That seemed to be an opportune time for him to relate what's happening and who that female was interrupting their nighttime romance. She promised never to tell anyone about this and after a quick breakfast, gave him a farewell kiss that he'd remember all his exciting day.

Joe arrived at the mall in an unmarked police car hours before it opened. He parked in a rather secluded area of the huge mall ramp. It was still somewhat dark when he crossed the ramp and walked down several flights of stairs to meet with mall security. The whole place seemed spooky, compared to the usual crowds converging on the popular retail mecca. It was eerie—quiet and lonely. About the only sound he heard were from his own footsteps as he proceeded down a narrow and winding stairwell.

A light beckoned from one of the doorways, letting Joe know he was heading toward the right gathering site. The door was slightly opened and he could already hear some talking within the meeting room as he approached. There was no need to knock or introduce himself. Having worked with this group so often over the past few weeks, he simply smiled, found a chair around the table, and very seriously told everyone in the group that they may be meeting with Mr. Beck and his bunch today.

All in the room listened intently to Joe as he unraveled his plan and expectations. While laying it all out, he scanned each face and badge, making sure all were authorized attendees and adequately informed and aware of the dread force about to descend on the mall.

In so doing, only one face seemed unfamiliar. It belonged to a rather unsociable person. Although he wore the correct tag on his shirt, signifying his credentials to attend, he also apparently was a stranger to the others and was somewhat isolated and seemingly reluctant to join in with any comments and suggestions.

Looking at the wall clock, Joe raised his hand for silence and announced that now was the time to spread out over the mall and report any suspicious personnel either coming or going. And he once again reminded those present of the great importance of keeping quiet about the special surveillance and arrest operation underway.

On their way out, Kavinsky made it a point to meet the newcomer.

His first thought was that this fellow conformed to all the standards of Hollywood: tall, dark and handsome. He appeared to be of Palestinian descent and a somewhat arrogant looking guy—not like a typical cop.

"Excuse me—but I couldn't help but notice you weren't participating much with the rest of us," said Joe. "Hope you got all the facts you need. By the way I guess I haven't met you before. Have you been working with us in the past and are you from around the metro area?"

"No sir…I'm with the new Home Security Department."

"Oh, the one that our president recently established?"

"Yes, the one and only. And it's been a tough job so far."

"How did you hear about our meeting? I thought it was only for a very select few from the DEA and FBI."

"The DEA invited me. I'm sort of new to the Twin Cities."

"What did you say your name is?" probed Joe.

"Pelot Jafid. My family originated from Bombay but I've been a U.S. citizen since birth."

"Jafed…Jafid," Joe repeated as if trying to memorize the name. "I think I've heard that name before. But like any guy in my job, we get an awful lot of names to keep in mind."

"Well…I hope I'm not getting in the way. I'm looking to be of considerable help to you and all our local authorities."

"Well you may be, you just may be," Joe said shaking his head in possible agreement.

"Do you have any questions about our plans discussed here so far?" asked Kavinsky.

"None whatsoever. I'm sure Beck will be caught—with all our help."

But as soon as Jafid left the room, Kavinsky immediately called Terry Johnson on his cell phone.

"Terry, do you know someone by the name of Pelot Jafid?"

"Pelot who? No, but the name Pelot rings a bell. Remember that bastard in the Bahamas who was reportedly killed by Zack Crimmons in a car accident?"

"You're right, he was called Pelot," Joe remembered. "But Jafid—have you ever heard of that name?"

"Never—but why do you ask? Aren't we suppose to be looking for our infamous enemy Beck?" "He may be one of them Terry. He says the DEA invited him to our secret meeting and that he's part of Home Security."

There was hesitation at the other end of the line. Joe waited for a response, but it was though Johnson set his phone down for a few minutes. When he returned to the phone however, his voice was rather shaky as he said, "Grab him Joe—and grab him now!"

CHAPTER 28

❀

Kavinsky ran out the door and almost spun his head around trying to find Jafid. Unfortunately, it was shortly after 10 a.m., meaning all the retail stores were now opened on all floors and crowds of waiting shoppers already began their rush to start buying. It was almost impossible to pick out any one person from this busy traffic.

Wondering how to spot Jafid, Joe recalled that when he left the room he put on a hat, pulled almost over his ears, and wore a dark suit with a red tie. The hat was a gray fedora with a slight crease near the front, much like the type the late Humphrey Bogart wore in movies of the '40s. In fact, if he was with actress Lauren Bacall, a star with Bogart in old flicks, he could quickly be recognized, Joe thought wishfully.

However, as luck would have it, when Kavinsky glanced down at the second-level there actually was a guy with a Bogart hat, going almost as fast as the mall walkers getting in their daily exercise. The only way he could catch up would be to take the elevator down to where Jafid would have to pass by. If timed right, he would be getting off the elevator at almost the same time Jafid would arrive there.

The elevator seemed extremely slow, however, as well as overcrowded. Shoppers squeezed in from almost everywhere. Kavinsky, in the middle of the elevator goers, could barely see the elevator door open on the 2nd level due to all the outgoing and incoming traffic and had to look over many heads to see the doors open. Despite all this, he was surprised when he nearly collided with Jafid almost the moment he stepped out of the elevator.

It reminded Joe somewhat of when he surprised Sarah shopping for shoes. He also felt like interrupting Jafid's rush to get through the maze of shoppers hurrying to leave the elevator by simply tapping him on the shoulder and saying "boo."

Instead he just said matter-of-factly, and rather quietly not to upset the crowd: "Mr. Jafid—you are under arrest!"

Jafid turned abruptly to face Kavinsky, and turned pale when he noticed Joe was holding both a gun and set of handcuffs.

The cuffs nearly hid the small gun since Joe was careful to cover most of it with his hand gripping the gun butt. He looked Jafid squarely in the eyes and commanded: "Let's go pal, you should have lots of company with your buddies and Beck in the police detention center."

Jafid's mouth dropped as he saw Joe's determined look. He tried to utter some resistance, but Kavinsky had already spun him around and cuffed him.

"Don't say a word…it may be used against you in court. You're no DEA or Home Security agent and don't try to pretend you are," said Joe almost pushing the startled Jafid into a secluded corner and beginning to frisk him. "I see you've got a weapon or two. Do you always carry sharp knives or is that something the Taliban trained you with? Or perhaps you need these when you meet your Beck bunch at the mall to disclose our plans." Before Jafid could respond, Kavinsky was back on his cell phone requesting police support.

By the time backup help arrived, Kavinsky had his captor ready to go with them. He was rather pleased to hear the arrested man screaming as he was being led away discreetly as possible out one of the mall's back doors.

"All hail to the Taliban—you will not destroy us, we will destroy you. No matter what you do we will ruin your plans," he shouted.

"Whew!" commented Joe as he wiped his brow and tucked away his .38. "How did he creep in to our strictly confidential meeting?" Overhearing this, Johnson, among the DEA who came to his help, replied: "there's been a leak in our system, Joe, and we've gotta find out who it is...and fast. I only hope he or she hasn't already spilled our plans to others."

"I don't think so Terry. We couldn't find any cell phone or other electronic communications systems on him, but we do believe he was on his way to let his cronies know what we're up to." Terry noted, "who knows, they may be some Osama operatives, often middlemen and dealers for the heroin industry who earn a fortune for their al Qaida terrorist network."

CHAPTER 29

At least, Johnson and Kavinsky felt more confident in knowing that there was now one less chance that their intricate scheme of catching Beck in the mall would be foiled, thanks to catching Jafid before he could tell his comrades about it.

"Now all we have to do is wait to hear from your piano-playing pal," noted Johnson grinning rather sarcastically.

But before Kavinsky could reply with a wise-crack response he was once again interrupted by the jingling of his cell phone. "What's with this damn phone? It won't keep quiet this morning—not even at night," he said recalling his calls from Salid. Let's both adjust our cell phones so they'll have a special sound if we see Beck," suggested Terry. "Set them for that alarm and vibrating tone we both have."

Kavinsky already was alarmed by a sudden call from his uncle. "Joe, we got more than the goods on Cermak and Loring. I saw Amad's notes and heard tapes—they're more involved than we thought." Joe said, "thanks unc. But I can't talk right now. Save it for me 'till I call you later today. Sounds very interesting."

To emphasize the importance of this, Al added, "Yeah Joe. Seems they're over in Bermuda fishing for all kinds of ways to find drug money and avoid U.S. taxes."

"They haven't changed their ways much, have they Al. Bermuda is a haven for escaping our tax laws...they can avoid them by hoarding their money there."

Joe had to suddenly click off when he saw Terry waiving to him as if there was an important news break. He quickly asked his DEA buddy "what's up?"

Terry replied, "There's been a report that a large van with a group of passengers just drove up to the mall's west-side parking ramp."

"So?"...asked Kavinsky wondering why this would excite his experienced undercover friend so much.

"So it matches the description of the wanted vehicle and—get this—it includes one lonely female passenger among a lot of males."

Kavinsky wasn't too shook over this report either. After all, he thought, the west entrance was on the way to where Pete was stationed at the piano.

"Great—keep tuning me into this, Terry."

"I sure will—but hopefully your piano pal will remember our catchy tune. You know...the 'You've Got Me' one. We're all set to close in on them the moment we hear it."

Kavinsky was left pondering over the report that there was only one female spotted. Does that mean Beck changed his woman disguise? if so, how will he now be dressed? And most importantly, how can authorities recognize him?

All these questions popped into Joe's mind as he caught a final glimpse of Jafid being led away. He immediately called Terry back and told him to question Jafid within the next few minutes to see if he could shed any light on what Beck actually will look like entering the mall.

"If there's only one female, it must be our gal Sal," Joe figured.

Meanwhile, Pete was posed over the piano keys with the rough sketch of Salid on top of his grand piano. But since he was paid to provide music for shopper delight and selling enthusiasm, he also knew he had to start playing immediately for his store boss and couldn't wait for Joe's terrorists to come through the doors.

He began with some peaceful renditions, including "Stardust" and "Deep Purple" and then went into mprovisations of "Without a Song" and "Somewhere Out There." He planned on doing Sinatra tunes shortly after that. This would help him lead into the "I've gotcha" melody when necessary, without arousing suspicion among those to be "gotten," he thought with a rather impish smile—unlike a serious musician.

At this time all surveillance cameras were focusing on the west wing doors, awaiting the entrance of the Beck gang. It seemed like an eternity before anyone used the doors, however, which was unusual for the typical startup of mall activity. But this wasn't a special bargain day for the mall and no holiday sales were being promoted, Joe reasoned.

The only people passing through the doors up to now were mostly moms with kids in strollers or ma and pa types wearing athletic shoes, ready to begin their daily walking exercise. A few small groups of young guys and gals also passed by, probably on their way to either buying something or perhaps starting their part-time seasonal jobs.

In fact, the authorities were getting downright tired, and impatient, waiting for some action. However, they did notice a man entering alone who stopped immediately after opening the doors. Something was unusual about him. He began looking all around as though making sure everything was just right to proceed on.

The guy just stood there as he gazed right and left and almost up to the ceiling. "What the hell is he looking for?" mumbled one cop.

"He could be their lookout," cautioned the other.

The suspicious-looking fella finally walked a short distance and began gazing at all the shoe racks. Also, at this time he put a cell phone to his ear—but very quickly put it back on his belt as though he heard what he wanted.

"That's it…I'll bet that's the go-ahead for Beck and the others to enter. The all-clear signal," said a DEA agent. He almost instinctively put his hand on his pistol, as though ready for combat. But there was another long wait before any sign of any possible action.

The agent in charge of surveillance motioned for the cameras to focus more on the doors and the background so he might also see some of those walking from the parking area before reaching the entrance. It was at this time that he noticed a small group assembling and heading toward the doors.

"Heads up everyone, this may be the people we're waiting for," he warned.

Just before reaching the doors from the ramp, however, the suspects broke off into groups of two-or-three. They could pass off as typical families or fellow shoppers entering the mall, like many newcomers to this edifice of retailing, gazing all about eager to observe its many special and various attractions.

CHAPTER 30

❀

While Kavinsky and Johnson were helping to interrogate Jafid, the mall spotters were especially alerted to look for the woman reported to be with the group. They almost gave this up, however, due to so many people coming through the entrance. They also thought it strange that most stopped shortly after entering, as though waiting for someone else to come. Finally a young lady, very fashionably dressed, opened the doors and, with a smile strolled over to the shoe displays.

No one would ever recognize her as Salid, not even the feds with the sketch and binoculars. She was most attractive and dressed like a model. Unlike the others, she very casually checked over some slippers and then examined a few high-heeled boots. There was no evidence whatsoever that this comely miss ever wore any religious robes or scarf over her pretty face.

In fact, her attire seemed most appropriate for the occasion. It fit in well with the latest styles displayed and emphasized her eye-catching figure. Moreover, her graceful walk around the displays indicated she was indeed a very refined person, and probably very wealthy. The few sales clerks around the area at this time surely regarded her as a prime sales target.

The police witnesses to all this wondered even more about when, if ever, Beck was going to show up. At this point, they wrote off the cute gal as just another curious shopper who accidentally got mixed in with the others. They were especially confused when a call came in from DEA spotters stating that all the group was now in the mall. There was no more expected. Beck either was among them—or didn't come.

The only other alternative was that Beck may have discarded his "dress" and was now one of the many male visitors walking about and headed toward his mysterious get-together with his gang of evil-doers.

Joe's jaw almost dropped, as he suddenly realized Pete at the piano wouldn't be able to signal the alarm needed to roundup this bunch if he had a hard time recognizing the girl. But it wasn't possible to reach Pete at this stage of events. Besides, it probably wouldn't help, since it would be too complicated explaining the changes in the sketch to the pianist who was now closely studying each line of the drawing of Salid's partially covered face.

As the spotters pondered over all this confusion, the woman proceeded into the main concourse and even approached the piano. Pete didn't bother to look up from the keyboard since he saw the woman come in and merely considered her as just another pretty face.

When he did look up from the keys, however, he was surprised to see that she had removed a handkerchief from her purse to touch-up some of her makeup and was gently using it on her face. It was a large hanky and almost appeared like a Muslim facial veil.

While improvising on the high notes with one hand, Pete took a pencil with the other and quickly tried drawing a similar veil on the face of the sketch before him. What he saw almost caused him to stop playing. It matched the sketch. It was her, the pianist suddenly realized, it was that woman the cops wanted!

To be certan, Pete again glanced at the sketch. Sure enough, the characteristics of the eyes, structure of the nose and even the small part of her forehead he could see were perfect matches of the drawing. In fact, he felt her eyes on him, almost pleading for him to start playing—or praying—for her. He began immediately.

Meanwhile Joe and Terry were compiling information they already received from Jafid and feedback they were getting from uncle Al on the cell phone about the latest happenings involving Cermak and Loring. They were now convinced that both the former police chief and medical examiner gave up their U.S. citizenship to protect their ill-gotten drug money in Bermuda and were fishing for more of it from around the reefs of that island.

But all their investigation came to a sudden halt. It was Joe who heard it first. He quickly recognized the music being played...the "I've Got You" tune coming from Pete's piano downstairs. "My God, Terry, Pete's telling us he sees Sal," exclaimed Kavinsky clicking his uncle off the cell phone, which he then quickly used to notify authorities on the main mall level.

While all this was going on, Pete was actually enjoying the catchy song he was playing. It was a great break from the regular store stuff he usually had to play to keep his boss happy. He added a few extra chords, bringing the tune so much up-to-date even Britney Spears would like to sing along. He smiled at many passersbys who began swinging with the tune. Some even came over to his piano to check the audio-tapes he wanted to sell.

But Joe and Terry weren't smiling when looking at the surveillance cameras. They still couldn't pick out anyone resembling Beck. Considering Joe actually saw Beck when he was tracking down drug lords in the Bahamas, this made him all the more upset in being unable to identify him from the other suspects now in the entranceway.

"Cripes, he's nowhere around," was all Kavinsky could mutter to Johnson.

"No one who even limps like him...no one with those cold green eyes...and no one with his stature. Maybe he's put on elevator shoes."

"Look long and hard, Joe, he's gotta be there," Terry urged. "His scouts went out first and I'm sure let him know everything was clear for him to make his appearance."

"Yeah, but he may have changed his mind, he's a slippery little son of a…" Joe didn't finish. He was suddenly distracted by the suspects as they began to move about, seemingly motivated by something or someone."

"Look Terry, do you see what I see? There's a guy in the center."

"God only knows what you see," shrugged Johnson grinning.

"That guy there—the smaller one. Is he holding a cigarette? It sure looks like it. And look, isn't there some smoke circling around his hand?"

CHAPTER 31

❀

Terry almost pushed Joe aside to look closer at the monitor.

"Maybe you're right. That's a crime in itself, the mall is a no-smoking place," he chuckled discounting Joe's seriousness.

But Joe continued, "No kidding Terry—Beck is an avid smoker. I've never seen him without a cigarette. He may be able to change his looks, but a guy like that could never break his smoking habit."

"Do you know what kind he inhales?" asked Terry to lighten the anxious moments. "Not really. But I'll bet it's the heavy nicotine ones. He's one of those die-hard smokers who are only loyal to the strong stuff—the ones that can usually do you in."

"Well, if you think he's the one, we better get him now, before he does everyone in," warned Johnson. "Yeah—but what do you suggest? He's extremely clever. If he has the slightest idea something's up, I'm sure he has some excellent strategy to get away."

"When he gets more into the mall we can always encircle him and his group," suggested Johnson. "Yeah—and have a shootout right there with everyone looking on…some strategy smart guy," mocked Joe.

"Well, do you have any better ones wise guy?"

"Wouldn't take much. But our support teams may have some answers. After all, we've already told them that Beck's arrived and is now in this place."

This reminded Johnson to get in touch with his team of enforcers again. "Close in on them now!" he commanded. "But do it discreetly without alarming any shoppers or anyone else around the area where they're at."

Joe then grabbed his cell phone and added, "and make sure the young lady with them is not harmed. She has lots of information for us."

The support team was ready to go. Most were undercover, including plain-closed cops. None wore any FBI, CIA, DEA or Homeland Security labels to reveal their identity. But Salid was still far ahead of them, and apparently leading the way to the secret site Beck selected for his get-together…wherever that might be.

As authorities closed in, they were suddenly interrupted by a high-pitched siren. It didn't take long to realize it was the mall's fire alarm that seemed to unnerve the entire retail complex, causing its hundreds of occupants to start racing toward the exits. Some even collided with one another in their dash to safety.

A voice over the intercom urged everyone to be calm, assuring that help was on its way. However, also on the way—to cause trouble—during all this sudden commotion was Beck's unholy group. Although most everyone seemed frightened and almost panicky, Beck appeared calm, still smiling and smoking.

However, Kavinsky and Johnson were also quite upset by all this mass confusion, wondering who set off the alarms and why? There was never a fire alarm rehearsal nor to their knowledge was there one planned for that particular day.

The most upsetting part of all this, though, was hearing the surveillance crew holler that the suspects they were watching had disappeared—both out of sight of the cameras and those assigned to follow them.

"The girl—get to the girl…She'll know where they are," yelled back Kavinsky.

"She's gone, too," they shouted in return.

Frustrated, Joe turned to Johnson and said, "take over here Terry; I'll go find her, and also find out what the hell's going on."

"Be careful Joe. It could be a setup. Everything seems so staged."

"Yeah, like someone masterminded all this. Someone who's apparently on top of all our planning."

"I don't think it would be Salid. She has everything to lose and nothing to gain. She indicated to you that she wants out of all this," noted Terry.

"I know, but who can we really believe and trust?"

In searching for the now scattered Beck group, mall security, agents and cops could only report that some were last seen racing up the escalators from the first to third floors. They added to the confusion by jostling shoppers rushing down to the exits.

"Oh great! they could now be on every level of the mall," said a disgusted Kavinsky throwing up his arms as if in despair.

But his concerns were lessened when a report suddenly came in that the woman suspect was still on first floor. In fact, she was standing near Pete's piano.

Joe lost no time in rushing to the piano site. From a distance he could see Pete chatting with the woman. He no longer was playing, of course, but seemed very calm and chatty now that the alarm scare was wearing off.

Kavinsky almost had to catch his breath before slowing down and walking casually up to the young lady, as if he was just out for a stroll.

He nodded to Pete, indicating everything's fine, and then introduced himself to the attractive but nervous woman next to the piano.

"Hi—I'm Joe Kavinsky. And you're?"…he purposely didn't finish hoping that she would complete the greeting.

"Salid, Mr. Kavinsky. Salid Ashid."

"Oh yes. We've talked before—but never met. I must say you're quite calm about all this confusion, with the fire alarm and all."

"Yes. I know there's no real concern. Instead I am admiring the fine drawing Pietro has. It almost looks like me," she said grinning at Pete.

Pete explained, "when the alarm went off I noticed her looking around and asked if I could give her directions to the best way out of here." He then made an excuse to go see how things were quieting down at the other mall exits, knowing Joe would like to discuss some police matters further.

This gave Kavinsky the chance he needed to talk confidentially with the striking brunette. "Do you know who set off the alarm?" he asked boldly, yet not wanting to intimidate her at the very start of his questioning.

"Yes, Mr. Kavinsky, it was Beck's men. An informer told them at the last moment of your plans and they immediately thought about sounding the alarm to help them hide and meet at another time. They carried smoke bombs in case this happened and gas masks if necessary. They are an evil bunch and won't be easy to catch."

She quickly added, "Believe me Mr. Kavinsky I am trying to cooperate with the police as much as possible. I deserve my pardon plea for the great risk I am taking. Please trust me, I had nothing to do with that poison in your coffee cup."

"My only intent was to hold the cup for your picture taking. Amad was the one with the poison. He asked me for the cup. I knew nothing of his plan to kill you."

Joe nodded, realizing the jury was still out on this matter.

He could only acknowledge, "Yes, I know your predicament and appreciate all your help. This will certainly be considered when your case comes up and should greatly help you," he assured the pleading young lady.

"What should I do? Where should I go? Beck will soon know I have been disloyal to him and will torture and kill me, like he did Amad."

"Stay with us now. I will have our support team protect you and make sure you have maximum security," assured Kavinsky as he clicked on his cell phone to his team now hunting down Beck.

While she waited for this protection, Joe took the opportunity to inquire if she had any idea where Beck may be during all this mall confusion.

He was surprised when she said, "he is waiting for me in the mall wedding chapel on third floor."

"Why there?," asked Kavinsky—wondering if that slime-ball wanted a quickie marriage with this young girl. Salid couldn't help but giggle over this. "It isn't what you think. He wants a big hall for his secret gathering. The only other place would be the school room where the mall's college is held on first floor."

"So he had this all worked out in advance. He must have been studying the mall for some time to know where best to conduct his dirty business."

"Yes, even his get-away plans," noted Salid.

"And what exactly is his business here, and his plans to escape?" asked Joe, eager to rush off to the wedding chapel.

"It's convenient to get all his global pals together to map out how to extend their drug trafficking and laundering more throughout the entire Upper Midwest. After all, you have international flights coming in right across from this area," she explained. "As for his escape, I was never brought into this. But it, too, is going according to plans."

"How come you didn't come here in your robes?. We hardly recognized you without something over your face," inquired Joe further. "Mr. Kavinsky, you don't understand…I was to be his bride if necessary. Even in parts of my country, the bride does not have to be hidden in robes if the groom desires. But as you know, I would never marry that snake."

Kavinsky was still amazed at all this as the support team walked off with Salid. He was convinced Beck indeed had every detail worked out. One detail he may have missed, however, was Salid's betrayal. Her chance for freedom apparently meant much more to her than any freedom that bird had for flying off to greater wealth.

"What do we do with her?" asked Johnson rubbing his chin as he pondered Salvia's plight.

"Let her go to the wedding," suggested Joe shrugging as though this was a needless question. "Without the bride, there won't be a so-called groom nor any of his groomsmen. I'm especially interested in who the best man will be aren't you?" Joe said in jest despite the serious nature of this matter.

"Well, we do want everyone to attend," agreed Terry.

"She's all set for the ceremony. So let's have her enter the chapel and act like nothing's happened," Joe said.

"We'd better be ready, too, if anything else does happen," Joe added. "Our security should encircle the chapel. But we've gotta make sure no one knows. But sneak up on them with the greatest silence, and caution. We don't want any shooting or noise that would further upset the shoppers."

"As far as we know, Beck doesn't suspect we're on to him. Right now he's probably waiting for his bride to show up." noted Terry.

Salid was almost up to the top level of the mall as Joe and Terry prepared to help the support team. They already told the team to surround the chapel as soon as Salid enters it.

Typical of some quick off-street wedding chapels, like those in Las Vegas, the planner of the phony wedding in the mall was asked to have no organ music nor anything fancy, not even decorations or refreshments.

Luckily the mall had rehearsed for terrorist attacks. As fire fighters converged on the downstairs, the upstairs cleared off somewhat from smoke and the wedding "guests" had no trouble reaching the chapel. When Salid showed up, hardly anyone noticed her as they mingled with their mostly bearded buddies to talk about some serious drug business.

All shut up almost at once, however, as a small man walked in and flicked cigarette ashes onto one of the dessert trays. "This has to be the weasel," commented Terry peering at the video monitor. "The guy's a nut. Anything goes with him, he could even toss a grenade at the minister and everyone would laugh."

"Yeah—he sure has them all under his control," Joe had to admit.

"Well let's call in our team and have them raid the joint," suggested Johnson. But just as Kavinsky was about to blow the whistle on Beck, the monitor went dead. It was completely black, as if it wanted nothing to do with all the evil on the tube.

"Get up there, Joe, and help harness them in before any get away," commanded Johnson. "We've waited a long time to see the color of that's guy's eyes."

"But that's what bothers me about all this Terry. Those eyes aren't green like Beck's. They look more dark, probably like the color of his soul."

CHAPTER 32

❀

Kavinsky was breathng hard when he arrived at the chapel doors. Almost wheezing, he wondered how such a heavy smoker like Beck could be running so much around the mall without nearly collapsing from the numerous cigarettes he inhales.

Joe barged into the chapel with his armed support team like a jealous suitor determined to bust up a wedding. All he could say as security flashed their badges and showed their guns was: "sorry folks, but this marriage is off."

As he looked around to see who he corralled, he noticed the little man who had been smoking so much. His first thought was that he was being used as a camouflage, to throw them off the trail. He went up to him and grabbed him by his suit collar. The fella was so puny that Kavinsky was tempted to turn him upside down and throw him out the chapel window.

As he was doing this, someone else was tugging at Kavinsky's arm.

"Joe, Joe let up—this is going nowhere. Beck has fled. He probably never was here," said the interfering deputy. "Can't you see—this was just probably to throw us off."

"It's that damn inside guy, the snitch in our own group…it's gotta be," said Joe raising his arms as if giving up on the whole damn operation.But the deputy chief comforted Joe somewhat by pointing out that all the others in the chapel were also on the wanted list. They caught them at their own trickery. Yet, the head mastermind of them all apparently was still on the loose. It was a bittersweet victory for Kavinsky.

He lowered his head, wondering who the hell it was that squealed.

While authorities wondered over who tipped off Beck, Johnson heard an unusual loud musical note on his cell phone from Joe alerting him that a suspicious man was seen running on the third level toward the exit escalator. The new phone alarm was the one Joe and Terry set up to signal special emergencies. The runner appeared to be small, and was shoving people aside if they got in his way, said Joe. But where the hell he was going—no one knew for certain.

"Do you know if he's reached the escalator yet?" asked the impatient DEA agent. "From what we can see he hasn't come that far," the surveillance spotter answered.

Johnson knew if Beck fled from the chapel at the time of the raid he should have arrived by now at the escalator, or even gone down it. His worse fear was that Beck found a hiding place before he reached the escalator and that somewhere, God only knows, this evil-doer was waiting for this manhunt to cool down so he could find a way to escape.

"Search the third floor thoroughly!" ordered Johnson. "Make sure every nook and cranny is inspected, but be extra careful—this guy is armed and ready to shoot it out."

Kavinsky, with gun-in-hand, assisted in the search. Mall workers and shoppers alike cleared the way for him as he showed off his police badge and cautioned them not to interfere. He even inspected the restrooms and phone stations, looked into the dark corners and hallways where teenagers often sneaked smokes and smooched girlfriends, but all to no avail. It almost seemed like Beck went up in smoke when the fire alarm was sounded.

Finally, Joe and Terry slowed down and spotted a diner near the escalator where they could catch a coffee and re-plan their strategy.

They figured there was no way Beck would have been able to get off the third level without the surveillance cameras picking him up.

"He's here somewhere Terry. Maybe even watching us from the kitchen in this restaurant," remarked Joe.

"You jest—but a rat can squeeze into even a very tiny hole quite quickly," responded Terry.

"What do we do—look for some rat poison?"

Johnson was all set to reply when his roaming eyes came upon an unusal mall attraction called the Musclemaster. He suggested,"well, if we really wanted to take a healthy break from all this, we probably should climb into that Musclemaster tube and get a massage."

"Is that what that's supposed to do?"

"Yep…according to the ads it's supposed to increase circulation and relieve muscular pain. Pulsating jets of temperature-controlled water travel back and forth over the body, at least that's what they advertise. And you don't have to get undressed or wet and come out relaxed and raring to go…if you can believe all that."

Joe was so curious he got off his stool and sauntered over to the Musclemaster display to know more about this interesting tube. He passed by a couple of tubes apparently being occupied and walked over to the check-in counter. However, even after ringing the bell for service several times, no one showed up.

Wondering what was keeping his pal, Johnson also walked the few steps to the display, still holding his coffee, and stood with Joe waiting for the manager.

Joe checked his watch and then began calling out: "Hello, hello…anyone here? We need some information." He didn't want to delay too much knowing Beck was on the loose.

To help, Terry peered around the corner of the door leading to the manager's office. He was horrified at what he saw. A man in his shirt sleeves, apparently the manager, was slumped over his desk, bleeding profusely. Terry called Joe and they both tried to revive the victim until realizing that he was dead

Kavinsky immediately called for assistance on his cell phone. He then went to the front of the Musclemaster display to signal where help was needed as the support team rushed to the scene.

While on his way past one of the tubes, Joe noticed it wasn't sealed properly like the others. It was opened slightly; allowing extra moisture to form on the glass cover and making it especially difficult for Joe to peer into the container. While doing this, he noticed how silent the massage noise became, despite the turbulent vibrating inside. He looked again, this time twice as determined to see what's going on. And this time he did see something—and that "something" saw him.

Beck!—The hunt was finally over. There the s.o.b was—lying on his back in the damn tube peering up at Joe with those cold green eyes.

This time there was no gun play. Beck could not possibly grab or use a gun that would fire in the moist mist around him in the narrow tube. Instead, Kavinsky simply kept staring at his eyes and then placed his .38 against the tube where the face of the drug lord, who terrified hundreds, now looked terrified himself.

"Come out, come out, wherever you are," said Joe recalling this little ditty from his childhood days. When Joe cocked his gun, Beck immediately motioned he was leaving the tube. The sight that emerged was awesome to behold for both Kavinsky and Johnson. The skinny little monster shook himself like a dog to dry off, and then smiled as if expecting a treat for out-maneuvering his captors for so long.

While Terry handcuffed the pathetic-looking drug dealer, he reminded him of his rights as Kavinsky proudly announced on a cell phone to his comrades in arms that the hunt was over and that Beck would finally be behind bars. You could almost hear the cheering as Beck was led out of the mall. Like the others arrested, he was escorted through the same rear entrance to avoid upsetting any shoppers and the many others who came from afar to enjoy the mall sights. However, this was a sight they shouldn't be seeing—but one which greatly delighted Joe and Terry.

As Joe pushed Beck's head down to get him into the police car, he gave him an extra shove thinking how ruthless this guy was, and hoped that he would be quickly brought to justice to pay for his many years of causing death and destruction.

CHAPTER 33

※

Cheers were also resounding around Kavinsky's police precinct at word of Beck's arrest. Chief Hermes was toasting the news with the many cops assigned to this case. About the only one missing was Dave Paulson.

As for Benjamin, while not snooping around on his beat, he was still trying to find out more about the report of Cermak and Loring being alive. The last he heard was that they were still busy fishing for money off the Bermuda shore.

The story on the capture of Beck and his gang wasn't officially released yet, so Al wasn't able to get a scoop on that—although he knew his nephew would give him a break on the story whenever possible. He was now focusing mostly on information from Beck's spy Jafid, who was being held in the St. Paul police detention center.

Authorities lost no time in letting Jafid know his boss Beck was arrested and that he had nothing to gain, and perhaps everything to lose, if he didn't cooperate in telling them what he knew about the infamous ex police chief and medical examiner. He told them his information was second hand, that he was obtaining it from an unknown source close to Beck. When asked who that source might be, Jafid said he wasn't sure but he understood it was within the St. Paul police force itself.

With that, the interrogators halted their high-pressured questioning. Instead, they looked at one another as though puzzled and amazed, wondering what lousy cop would dare stoop to divulge confidential police information to a creep like Beck.

As this was happening, doc Loring was busy scooping as many water-logged bills that he could find floating around the site where Zack Crimmons went down in the ocean. He shouted obscenities when Cermak got in his way with a large hook enabling him to seize the money faster from the water.

The containers they had on board their sailing rig were being rapidly filled with money of many different denominations. They had to fish out the floating bills very discreetly as they didn't want Bermuda authorities interfering. Most, however, stayed below their reach in the ocean depths apparently with Zack after his suicide plunge. He used heavy bags of money to keep from resurfacing. But some of the bags broke, allowing bills to rise to the surface helping to indicate where Zack jumped.

Interpol, the international police force, was notified of this almost as soon as Jafid finished informing local authorities. They in turn contacted appropriate Bermuda authorities who began an investigation. They knew from records filed during the suicide approximately where the money-searchers may be and sent out a search party to check into this. Al was at St. Paul police headquarters when Interpol issued a report advising local authorities that Loring and Cermak would soon be rounded up for further questioning.

It was still uncertain in everyone's mind as to what would be done with the money once the suspects were taken into custody. Al figured it would be good PR for all involved to give it to some needy organization. He was sure there would be lots of people trying to claim it. But he hoped and prayed that the Taliban wouldn't get their filthy hands on it.

Benjamin was still committed, of course, to keeping any news concerning the possible whereabouts of Cermak and Loring under-wraps from his fellow press associates until all this could be confirmed officially by U.S. authorities.

As chief Hermes noted, if they changed their citizenship then they would most likely be held and tried in Bermuda, unless special extradition was agreed upon by all the necessary authorities involved for returning them to the U.S. This was especially complicated, of course, since Bermuda is under British domain.

"But they're alleged criminals—with direct ties to the underworld and I'm sure will not be allowed to keep any of that water-soaked money," explained Hermes. The chief returned to his desk, seemingly perplexed. Wiping his brow he said almost to himself in earshot of Al, "I need some reinforcements. I still don't know where Paulson is. All this time he's been gone—just when we need him most."

"Last I saw him he was helping to get names of possible Beck conspirators from Amad's files," recalled Al.

"With Joe so wrapped up in this case and out of the office so much—and Paulson absent and Amad gone—I have all I can do to manage the many other affairs of this police department." complained Hermes. Well," comforted Al, "maybe I can help by continuing to write down those suspect names that Dave was getting from Amad's files." Al also couldn't help but think of the great scoop he'll have and how this could make for a super front-page headline story.

Interpol was slow in submitting information regarding the status of Cermak and Loring, despite the anxiety and impatience of local authorities. However, most realized there would be numerous channels involved in officially releasing such incriminating data, especially considering all the international technicalities and protocol procedures involved.

Benjamin, already using up almost a month of vacation from his newspaper, was also getting very impatient to get back to his newsroom again. This, and the fact that he was gone a lot from Kay and home, caused him to grumble while sorting through the remainder of Amad's files. Al was nearly finished noting the names of those listed by Amad, who were most apt to be associated with Beck, when one nane in particular stood out and startled him so much he nearly fell off the stool he was sitting on.

The name was Paulson—Dave Paulson! Benjamin's first reaction was why in hell would he be mentioned? Doubting that it was the same Dave Paulson that worked next to Amad, Benjamin quickly looked over the scribbled report. What he read he had to read over and over again. It was! It was David L. Paulson, the police detective that was working with Amad to help capture the drug king. This couldn't be true—but could it? Such upsetting thoughts kept crowding Al's mind.

He almost instinctively reached for the phone to alert his nephew about this. But Joe also was difficult to track down, and after many rings of his cell phone Al clicked off. It was lucky he did so, since a couple seconds later a call came in to Benjamin's cell phone. It was from Paulson. But Al didn't click onto the call...Dave was leaving a message on his voice mail.

"Al, I thought I'd catch you at the precinct. Just thought I'd let you know that I'll be able to follow through with searching Amad's files. Don't do any more at this point until I come back in the next couple of days," Paulson requested.

Since Benjamin didn't have caller ID, there was no indication where Paulson was calling from. He phoned his wife Kay to find out if Dave tried calling their home. If so, there would probably be a phone number where he could be reached on the home caller ID monitor. But Kay said there were no calls from Paulson.

As Al was about to make some copies of Amad's lists relating to Paulson, chief Hermes rushed in and announced that he finally heard back from Interpol.

"Good news Al, both Loring and Cermak are behind bars," announced the smiling Hermes. "What's more, they've arrested an accomplice who was with them in Bermuda. I don't know who that is yet...perhaps someone we've never met."

Benjamin nodded his head and said "great," thinking however that the accomplice could indeed be Paulson.

When Al returned home, Kay said he had a phone message from Joe. "He noticed on his caller-ID that you tried to call him. He said he's been busy bringing a lot of guys to justice and that you'd know what he's talking about."

"I sure do. And there should be one more coming," said Al.

Kavinsky was much too busy to respond to many phone callers, especially calls from some inspector at the post office who Joe figured just wanted to be in on the Beck arrests. He made sure, however, to answer the call coming from "Sal."

"Mr. Kavinsky I'm at the U.S. Marshal's office. Please help me, as you and the others promised in return for my plea bargain, I said I could also give you names of those who helped Mr. Beck try to escape. Let me know if you now need this. I must hang up now," she said nervously.

Joe appreciated this very brief, but to the point, message. After telling Terry about this call he dashed off to the U.S. Marshal's office at the Twin Cities federal building to visit Salid. He assumed she would be with marshal deputies, maybe even having coffee or at least being shown some courtesies. Instead, she was behind bars in the dark basement of the Post Office building.

"Salid?" asked Joe, looking at a frail young lady who appeared frightened in her new surroundings. She lost much weight and was very pale due to the Beck manhunt. The lockup room contained only three cells. Salid was all alone in hers. The others were empty. "We have some mail fraud prisoners coming tomorrow," explained the assistant marshal. "We'll probably have to transfer this young lady to another lockup," noted the marshal.

"I must remind you, marshal, she's protected by the U.S. Attorney's office—and receiving preferential treatment due to a plea bargain agreement," cautioned Joe. He then was ushered to her cell where he sat down on a cot with Salid to talk.

"Mr. Kavinsky, I have news for you," Salid said for openers.

"Good—or more bad?" questioned Joe attempting to grin.

"I'm afraid it's more bad, since it involves someone I believe you know."

"Who's that?" Joe said, almost hesitant to ask.

"Your friend David Paulson."

"What about him?"

"He was helping Beck. He was with us at our meetings sometimes. He also received information from Amad and was working with dishonest law officers…I believe a Mr. Cermak and a Doctor Loring."

"Yeah—I know them well. Dave's been missing. Do you know where he went?"

"I was told by Amad, before he was killed, that they both fled to the island of Bermuda to retrieve some drug money."

Joe sat back and looked Salid directly in her pretty eyes. "Are you positive about all this? If this is so, Paulson's career would be ruined and he would be regarded as a traitor. He had everything going for him, and this could destroy him."

"I am very sure your man Paulson is one of them."

Joe sighed deeply. He was now giving up all hope that there was anything good about Paulson. He had thought for a while that Dave had changed his ways and was going straight. After all, Dave helped Terry save Kavinsky from being killed less than six months ago when Cermak and Loring were trying to obtain information from Joe about where the drug money was hidden.

It was clear now that this was just a cover up for Paulson, allowing him to get closer to influential sources who could benefit him financially—such as Beck as well as others who knew how to obtain lots of money quickly by drug trafficking and laundering.

And of course, sitting next to Amad at work may have been all part of Paulson's clever strategy, allowing him to keep close tabs on illicit drug operations.

Whatever the situation, the alarm was now out to get Paulson as soon as possible, including an APB all-points-bulletin sent out by Joe.

But despite this flurry of activity, Kavinsky was still able to find time for his uncle Al. In fact, the next day they got together for lunch to relax a little. Joe wanted to thank his uncle, of course, for his help in keeping most of this out of the press until the time was right and helpful for authorities—and the nation.

While sipping their favorite brew, even though still on duty, Joe announced to a surprised Al that he now could start breaking the news regarding Beck.

"Hope we haven't gotten you into lots of hot water over this unc. If any of your peers give you any heat refer them to me or the chief, or for that matter even Terry. You might say, withholding information like this was for the good of all of us."

"You're damn right Joey. God only knows what they were planning up here. Who would suspect that they would choose an Upper Midwest meeting place like our mall. However, the more I think about it, this was awfully convenient considering the close proximity to the international airport for coming and going unnoticed. Plus they could be easily lost mingling with all the shoppers."

"What's your next step nephew? Any plans for a break in all this and some extra attention to your wonderful bride?" Benjamin inquired teasingly.

"Glad you asked unc," said Joe as he took another drink of beer.

"I'd like to spend lots more loving time with Sarah. However, I also may have to fly over to Bermuda as a witness if they try Cermak and Loring over there."

"What about Paulson?"

"From what I understand, they'll probably have to try him in the U.S.—right here in fact. He's still a U.S. citizen unlike the others."

"When will you be going?" inquired Al. "Probably soon, the Bermuda authorities want to talk to me," Joe replied with a rather reluctant shrug.

Sarah asked the same question when her busy husband arrived home. She was getting rather impatient for him to get off this case as soon as possible.

It seemed hard to know when he was going or coming these days. Joe, too, longed to catch up on his loving and wanted to stay home to do more. He was upset whenever the home phone rang, thinking it might be his orders to report to Bermuda. So far, most of the calls were from telemarketers.

But, as expected, the moment he got in bed with Sarah and put his arms around her to begin making love the phone rang again.

"If that's your friend Sal…tell her to go to hell," remarked Sarah angrily and quite loudly— ignoring her rhyming words.

Joe would have preferred to hear from anyone other than the voice on the other end of the phone.

"Joe, chief Hermes. You'd better go to Bermuda tomorrow. The Bermuda authorities just notified me that they'll have our suspects in jail, and that Paulson will be among them, even though he's not a Bermuda or British citizen."

Kavinsky held the phone halfway to his ear as he peeked over at Sarah who was now propped up against her pillow gazing at her watch waiting for her lover to return to bed.

As Hermes provided the complex details about the trip, also mentioning that a DEA agent named Dana will be traveling with him, Kavinsky yawned and winked at Sarah and kept saying "yeah, yeah" while counting the seconds when the chief would hang up.

Flying to Bermuda took longer than to the Bahamas where, as Joe vividly recalled, most of the drug problems in this case originated.

The Bahamas also was a stopping off point for drug trafficking to virtually everywhere in the world.

But Bermuda seemed much cleaner, at least cleaner than the criminal element he encountered in Nassau. While landing at the Bermuda airport, he could see numerous clean white roofs of the homes around that area that helped keep rain water so pure that many residents reportedly pumped it into their homes for drinking.

And it was easy to remember whose island this really belongs to. The airport was nearly surrounded by British military aircraft, and the shoreline dotted by aircraft carriers and other large ocean vessels flying the English flag. As Joe and his DEA partner descended the steps of the airliner, he also noticed a very tall lighthouse about a mile away. For some reason it was already throwing a beacon to incoming ships. He checked his watch and surprisingly found that this already was Bermuda dinner time and that fog was moving in quickly.

He and Dana hailed a cab and checked into the Hamilton Beach Hotel. Although the cab driver spoke like he was from Brooklyn, he seemed well adjusted to steering his cab like the British do on the right side rather than the left and easily swerved around the many tourists riding their mopeds in and out of traffic.

"Visitors are our lifeblood. We go out of the way to get out of their way," explained the friendly cabby.

Kavinsky and his DEA associate spent little time checking in. Dana called his fellow DEA agents at the Hamilton prison and let them know they had arrived and would meet with them for dinner.

The restaurant, on a side street patrolled by police bedecked in decorative white jackets, kingly hats and blue pants, offered a wide variety of seafood specialties that caught Kavinsky's eyes. He could also see considerable boating activity from the panoramic picture window next to his table. While eating and chatting with the others, Joe also noticed the rough waters tossing many of the ships about as they approached the giant reefs nearby the shore line.

With such an interesting view, he was somewhat distracted at times until the group started talking about what to do with Paulson.

"We'll take you to him later this evening. Bermuda attorneys are representing the others, but your man is alone and awaiting transportation back to the states," said the DEA Bermuda director to Kavinsky and Dana.

"We've talked to the airlines and they'll have him in a special section. I'm sure you'll want him cuffed."

"That won't be necessary," interrupted Joe. "I've known him for some time and he's really not a violent man."

"We've already frisked him…he has no weapons," they noted.

"By the way, Mr. Kavinsky, Paulson said he'd like to see you after our dinner. He didn't say why. I told him I'd let you know. He's now in one of our small jails a few miles from here just off Main Street."

After finishing some vintaged wine and enjoying steak soaked with special Bermuda rum smothered, of course, with Bermuda onions, Kavinsky wiped his face with the warm towel provided by his courteous waiter and prepared to visit Paulson.

The DEA director left the café with Joe and declared softly but quite seriously, "we're very sure Mr. Kavinsky that Mr. Paulson is indeed the mole in your organization."

It was dark when Joe arrived at the jail house. Even the taxi driver had difficulty finding the tiny brick building with bars on the windows. Joe noticed a flicker of light behind a window near the front door and knew someone besides the prisoners was on hand.

Upon exchanging greetings and showing his badge and credentials, Kavinsky was invited in and led down a narrow corridor, lined with cells and what appeared to be down-trodden imprisoned men, to an isolated corner where Paulson was being caged.

Despite all this gloom, Paulson managed a slight smile on seeing Kavinsky. "Howdy friend, seems your police partner got himself into a heap of trouble," he said for openers peering through the bars. "Did you have a nice trip to this paradise?"

"Why, Dave…why?" was all Joe could reply.

Both sat down on the flimsy cot in the jail cell near a dirty toilet bowl, and Paulson then leaned over and put his head down as though in utter despair.

"Money, Joe, and lots of it. I was being paid off by Beck after Amad arranged to have me as their inside man…inside our precinct, that is."

"But you were our man—we brought you into everything we were doing to catch him. We trusted you Dave."

"I know, I know," he agreed nodding his head. "Cermak and Loring also made it attractive for me to side in with them. The way they made it sound was that I would be as wealthy as them after all this was done.

"What happens next Joe?" he asked looking up at Kavinsky with almost pleading eyes.

"Guess you have to come back to the Twin Cities with us Dave. They want to officially charge you and go from there."

After further discussion on the process foreseen in judging and sentencing, Joe suggested that Paulson contact a lawyer immediately upon getting back to defend himself. He figured Dave already knew the procedures having gone through this with so many of the criminals he helped to catch back home.

Getting a good night sleep in a strange room, yearning for Sarah, and listening to some loud boom music coming from the next room, all helped to make for a restless night for Joe. Most of the time, however, he was thinking about what was in store for Paulson and Salid. Both seemed rather pathetic in their strange and isolated locations, and, who knows, perhaps somewhat mistreated in their captivity.

Joe had no time for breakfast or even a cup of coffee when he awoke early the next morning to get ready for his trip home and busy agenda. To add to his upset, the phone next to his bed began ringing so loudly that he nearly shouted into the receiver.

"Yeah—what do you want?"

The caller at the other end, hesitated as though afraid to talk to the voice yelling at him.

"Is this police lieutenant Kavinsky?"

"Yes," said Joe in a much softer tone.

"This is sergeant Kinney from the Bermuda city jail. I have some bad news for you."

Joe's first thought was that something happened to Sarah. He sat down on his bed, mussed up by his excessive tossing about, and waited for the message with his fingers crossed.

CHAPTER 34

❀

"I'm sorry to report that prisoner David Paulson is dead. He apparently committed suicide."

Kavinsky didn't bother to shower or shave in his rush to get to the jail house. But by the time he arrived, the body had already been removed and was being prepared for return to the states with Joe. To find out more about how he died, Joe quizzed the constable at the jail and the jailer who last saw Dave alive. They did note some knife marks on the body and told Joe they wanted to check these out further since although Dave's sharp steak knife had blood stains on it, he would have had great difficulty inflicting such a wound on himself.

Within only a few hours, Joe was on a plane again—this time heading back to the Twin Cities. However, instead of returning with the arrested suspect sitting next to him, he was very much alone. His associate, DEA agent Blaine, remained in Bermuda for the international arraignment of Loring and Cermak. Paulson who was supposed to fly back with him as a passenger in handcuffs was instead in a casket in the cargo area of the airliner. At least there no longer was any need for him to be handcuffed, thought Joe.

In some way, however, Kavinsky felt he wasn't alone. He kept his fingers on the knife under his jacket that supposedly was used to kill Dave. It was still stained with Paulson's blood and, if necessary, could be evidence for the DNA lab. After all, Paulson probably knew more than anyone about the inside operations of the drug "business" around Minnesota and elsewhere. But perhaps he knew too much for his own good. Joe was sure Dave just didn't seem to be the type to commit suicide.

During the long flight home, Kavinsky also couldn't help but be reminded that this was the second time he was returning from Bermuda under very somber conditions. The first was not long ago when he and his bride returned from that island after being notified of her dad's death.

Upon landing and watching the casket being carried into a hearse waiting on the airport strip, Joe called Sarah letting her know he was now on his way to the precinct to check in and report on his trip, and then, thank god, he should be back home to what he fondly referred to as their wedding nest.

But it wasn't quite that easy he found out when recalling his Bermuda experiences with chief Hermes. For one thing, a detailed report had to be made out on the current status of Cermak and Loring, as well as the circumstances of Paulson's rather mysterious death. Moreover, before leaving the precinct he was asked by Hermes to check with U.S. marshals at the federal building in downtown St. Paul regarding the status of Salid's detention there. It was "absolutely necessary" reminded Hermes that plea bargain agreements are honored by all authorities for this "brave little lady." Kavinsky didn't complain, however, since this was on his way home.

But to get to the marshals, he first had to enter and pass through the Twin Cities Post Office headquarters and then take an elevator down to the depths of the federal detention area. Plus, he had to sign in again and list his credentials along with writing down his badge number. Ever since the World Trade terrorist attack it seemed like everything had to be done in triplicate, Joe felt.

CHAPTER 35

But it took only a few minutes before he was led to Salid's cell again. This time he found her to be less apprehensive about what was going on. But still Joe felt obliged to know for sure if she was receiving the help she was promised by betraying Beck and assisting with his capture. She was also told about Paulson's arrest and death. Stunned, Salid put her head on Joe's shoulder and began to weep. He knew she wasn't faking. As his shirt became wet from her tears, he put his arm around her and once more assured that he personally would see to it that she would be well treated and defended.

Before departing, he was advised by marshals that Salid would be appearing before a judge within the next two weeks. Further, she would be alone in her defense, having no allies or relatives at the arraignment since she was a native of far-off Karout, a desert town in Pakistan. In fact, Joe and chief Hermes would probably be her only witnesses attesting to the terms of the plea bargain.

Kavinsky wiped some of the tears from Salid's eyes as he updated her on this. He felt like kissing her goodbye, but controlled his desires for affection by thinking of all the loving and hugging he'll be getting soon from his beloved Sarah.

However, his rush to get home was once again delayed. On his way out of the federal building he was startled by a loudspeaker calling out his name. His first thought was that he forgot to add something to the marshal's sign-in sheet and would have to return once again to the bottom level of the old building.

The loudspeaker said simply: "Mr. Joseph Kavinsky, Mr. Joseph Kavinsky...please check with the postal inspector before leaving the building. Repeat, Joseph Kavinsky please contact the postal inspector."

Joe figured the postal inspector's office might be nearby, usually in an office near the Post Office counters where stamps are sold and customers get advice from postal clerks. It took longer to find, however, since the windows of the counters were still closed so early in the morning and there was no one around to ask where the inspectors hang out.

Although Sarah mentioned the name of a postal inspector some time ago who supposedly was trying to get in touch with him, it slipped Joe's mind. He was all set to depart from the federal building, upset over why the hell it wasn't marked better, when he accidentally noticed a door with a big sign "Postal Inspector" on it.

There was no need to knock. The moment he touched the knob the door opened slightly and Joe assumed that he was welcomed to come in. Fortunately there were several people at their desks. One got up to greet Kavinsky, a Jerry Donovan, a name that sounded rather familiar to Joe. Donovan smiled broadly and told him they've been waiting to talk to him for some time. The reason they knew he was in the building was due to the marshal's requirement of informing all occupants about visitors arriving before the federal building is officially opened for business. Perhaps this was a new rule after the horrible bombing of the Oklahoma City federal building, Joe reasoned.

"Do you realize we've been trying to contact you or your wife for weeks now and haven't had a response?" asked the head postal inspector.

"I'm sorry—I've been awfully tied up with running down some criminals and couldn't tear myself away," explained Joe, realizing that he was shading the truth somewhat.

"Well, I'm glad you're sitting down Mr. Kavinsky, because what I'm about to tell you may floor you and your wife."

"How the hell does my wife fit into this?" asked Joe frowning.

"Very much, since it relates to her father. We we're advised that he used the mails just before he was reported to have committed suicide."

"And so…? quizzed Joe. "Is that a crime in your books?"

"Could be, but for your sake I hope there's something to gain from it all."

"Guess you'll have to be more explicit sir," said Joe wondering where this was all leading."

"I'll explain it the best I can," said the director, getting up from his chair, putting on his glasses, and walking over to his desk to check some papers.

"The mail sent from Bermuda to your house contained a couple of checks. However, they were burned somewhat in a fire that broke out in one of our mail trucks, a fire that destroyed most of the letters and other materials intended for deposit in mail boxes along your neighborhood. Our driver tried desperately to put the fire out. Needless to say, there were only a few items left that weren't completely destroyed. Among these was an envelope addressed to a Sarah and Susan Crimmons. I believe Sarah is your wife?"

"Yes, and Susan is her sister. Do you have the letter?" asked Joe impatiently.

"I have it…somewhat. Everything in that truck was either severely burned or smoke damaged. In the case of that letter, smoke got to it—leaving it soggy and nearly unreadable along with the checks."

With that, the director picked up a grimy, darkened envelope and shook out the contents. "See what I mean. Yet, this was the only piece of mail that you might say survived the fire."

Joe got up and came over to the desk to examine the envelope remains. There was still a strong smoke smell. The director beckoned Joe to come closer. "You'll find the words very interesting Mr. Kavinsky, despite being difficult to read…especially notice the checks."

"Keep in mind, however, this is a matter for Sarah and her sister."

When Joe tried picking up the fragile, partially burned papers they almost fell apart. He had to squint and look closely to read what was written.

"You needn't ruin your eyesight Mr. Kavinsky. I can tell you that the note seems to be an apology from Zack Crimmons to his daughters and the checks a peace offering. Now, if I were you I'd return to your chair and sit down. As you'll note, there are two checks—one for Susan and one for your wife."

"For how much?" asked Kavinsky urging the director to get to the point of this suspenseful discussion.

CHAPTER 36

❊

"Each check, Mr. Kavinsky, is for twenty-million-dollars."

The room became suddenly very silent. Not another sound was heard. It was though something fell over the conversation and muffled it to a point that only an echo prevailed—the echo saying over and over again in Joe's mind: "twenty million dollars, twenty-million-dollars."

The postal inspector broke the silence by adding, "but that's only on paper. Although, surprisingly, the paper is still somewhat readable and authentic."

"It's for real?" Joe asked hardly believing what he heard.

"Perhaps some of it, and maybe more. But there are some complications," warned the inspector.

"Like what?"

"In addition to the fact that the checks are very soiled, they also represent 'dirty money'. From what we're advised by our investigators much of it comes from illegal drug money."

Before Joe could respond, the inspector put up his hand to ward off his comments and said much more investigating still needs to be done. "It took so long to reach you that during the time we were waiting, we checked into the possibilities of what your wife might be entitled to. She, of course, will have to know first about such details—this legally concerns her of course."

He continued, "perhaps she will want to consult with a financial advisor as well as an attorney. I understand Zack Crimmons was a lawyer and may have had a separate account for his legal business...that is separate from any of his illegal income. If so, I presume that portion would rightfully be yours—I mean your wife's."

Kavinsky left the federal building stunned and filled with both hope, joy and perhaps disappointment. When he told Sarah of this, they both hugged one another for support and prepared to endure whatever time and effort would be involved in further investigations. The federal postal inspectors had the authority to hold the checks in tight security until such investigations were completed.

In the meantime, Joe and Sarah sought help from those acquainted with such complex financial affairs as well as with lawyers and, of course, bankers with some of Zack's money in their vaults. Sarah spent much of her time just keeping track of all the expenses they were going through because of this, wondering also what terrible taxes they would be facing even if they got some of the money.

It became so upsetting that they had difficulty sleeping at night, although Joe wasn't too concerned about this since it allowed more time to get in more love-making. After several months, however, they got back to their routines and began thinking of other things—including having a family.

It was when they went to bed early one evening and were snuggling up to one another that Sarah made an announcement to her lover.

"Joe, we're going to have a baby."

Kavinsky was beside himself. He was so happy, in fact, that he danced around the bed as Sarah laughed at his antics.

The celebration stopped abruptly, however, when the phone rang loudly near their bed. He wanted at first to ignore it, but knew it might be another police call that needed immediate attention.

Before he reached for the phone, Sarah propped herself up on her pillow and, with her hands on her hips, warned: "If that's your girl friend again, tell her to butt out."

Joe chuckled and grabbed the phone. The caller was a woman, however, but one with a very business voice representing the attorney general's office.

"Mr. Kavinsky? Joseph Kavinsky?, she asked making sure she was talking to the right party.

"Yes maam, I'm he," responded Joe trying to talk straight while still almost hyperventilating from Sarah's baby news.

"May I talk to your wife?" This was so surprising that all he could do was pass the phone to Sarah and say with a frown: "It's for you."

Sarah listened intently, her smile widened and then she beamed—almost more than she did when she told him about the baby.

Joe quit clowning around and anxiously waited for her to hang up. But when she did, she arose from the bed and began dancing with him.

"Hey, what's up?" he asked almost out-of-breath. "You're supposed to be taking it easy with the baby coming and all."

"Joe, honey, we're not only about to have a baby—we're about to have five-million-dollars to spend on her—or him," she rejoiced. "The authorities have checked it all out. They found that daddy had ten-million set aside in a trust that was made out years ago when he was still in his legal and lawful practice...five for me and five for Susan that may help in Susan's defense."

With that, they embraced again and began thinking about the many great and wonderful things they can buy for the baby and get ready for the birth—things that are cheerful and gentle—the farthest thoughts from their past experiences of dread and terror.

In fact, they began dancing around the bed again as though the baby was already in their arms. Even Stella the dog seemed happy, and began her own type of prancing, and perhaps canine dancing, with them—until hitting a lamp with her long wagging tail.

And, of course, the gleeful couple also planned to go back to the super mall as soon as possible. But this time, Sarah warned, for some "very, very serious shopping" without any distractions—and especially without any coffee breaks.

The End

0-595-26356-9

NORMANDALE COMMUNITY COLLEGE
LIBRARY
9700 FRANCE AVENUE SOUTH
BLOOMINGTON, MN 55431-4399